The Lost Song of Miriam Landry
Rob Cooke

I0618914

Thank you, Kyra, Kevin, and Daniel.

Thank you, Gloria for the inspiration.

Thank you, Stephen Center for allowing me to finish at your shelter.

Thank you to my Beta Readers, Pam Van Allen and Debbie Schoeningh for you kind and harsh words. There are way too many people to thank, personally but somewhere Miriam's struggle for survival became intertwined with mine. If you knocked me down with the sole intentions of setting me up to knock me down again. Thank you. Miriam is a survivor, and so am I.

Here's the proof.

Prologue:
Shreveport, Louisiana
1993

"I've made so many bad decisions in this deal folks call life." The woman said to the empty room. The silence reverberated.

She looked over her paneled wall, noticing the gold-plated record. She gawked at the old photographs. A smile came across her face. It might have been a sad smile, as drops of moisture formed in her eyes.

"I never knowed how talented I was. Guess I needed to step out of da life to realize it." She poured herself a glass of lemonade and grabbed that beat-up Stella guitar her friend gave her years ago, going to her front porch.

She twisted the pegs on her guitar, tuning to open G. She slid an old piece of pipe on her finger. It was her favorite slide, one she had since she was a teenager, one from the thirties. The pipe slid up the strings as she picked the strings with her right hand. She smiled, still with the tear in her eye. "I never knew I was worth so much more."

As her aging fingers strummed the guitar, the years lost came flooding back to her. She brought the swamp to her Northern Louisiana home.

*   *   *

"I'm looking for a woman." A well-dressed man told the cab driver at the Shreveport airport. Sporting a short, fashionable goatee, dark sunglasses, and a gray fedora, and speaking in an African accent. The man should have been more specific. The cab driver smiled at the foreigner. "I know where to takes you. I gonna take

Cory laughs. "After you, Jason."

Within moments, they walk together into the light leaving Ronnie and Rick to take the first steps in living their dream.

Judith Ann McDowell is a novelist with several finished books. When not working on a manuscript, Judith, along with her husband, likes to travel to different cities such as New Orleans to talk with people about voodoo and to talk with those who have experienced firsthand true hauntings.

Judith is the mother of four grown sons, Guy, David, Rhett and Nick, and lives in the Pacific Northwest with her husband Darrell and their two Pekingese Chi and Tai and three cats Isis, Lacy and Keefer.

Judith is at present working on her next novel.
Visit her website: https://judithamcdowell.wixsite.com/jamcdowell

CHAPTER ONE

SOMEWHERE IN THE PACIFIC NORTHWEST 2018

"I know this is none of my business, Ronnie, but I don't understand why you want to waste money on this mausoleum when you have a perfectly good room at home, in a house that is maybe not as big, but certainly every bit as nice." Raquel Westerlyne looks around, her balled hands resting on her slim hips.

"I'm not a child, Mama. In case you haven't noticed, I've grown up. I want my own home and, someday, when the time is right, a husband and children. I need a big house to fit them all in."

"Have you even considered what it is going to cost to heat this place in the winter? You know how bad the winters can get here in the Pacific Northwest. Not only that, I don't see how you expect to do your job all week and still take care of a five-bedroom, three-bath house. I don't know what was in my brother's mind to leave you this house anyway."

"I think this house is unique," she said, flipping long, silky black hair over one shoulder as she opens her purse lying on the dark, mauve-colored island in the huge kitchen. Withdrawing her phone, she clicks off pictures as she makes her way through the house. "Remember, this house has been in a lot of movies. I think I'm lucky to live in a famous house."

"Oh yeah, you're really lucky to live alone in a house that sits in the middle of 100-acres of forest."

"Oh, stop worrying. A lot of people would give their all to live here."

"You can be sure, the ones wanting to live here would be the ones who frequented the kind of parties that went on here."

Ronnie looks at this tall, slender woman dressed in a pair of designer jeans and a teal-colored, short-sleeved shirt. At fifty-two years old, she has to admit this woman, with her thick auburn hair styled just right to frame her heart-shaped face, the dark green eyes, and great genes that she inherited, allowing her to keep the slim figure so mandatory in the modeling business, is a very beautiful woman.

"Uncle Cory was a very famous actor. I doubt he spent much time in this house since he was on location most of the time. His gay life was his business. Had he lived a straight life, I am sure he would have had his son or daughter inherit the house. However, since he didn't, I, Veronica Westerlyne, now live in the house that I have always loved to visit since the first day you and Dad brought me here."

"Yes, you were his favorite to spoil. By the way, you *have* heard the rumors about this house being haunted." Raquel watches her waiting for her reaction.

Ronnie laughs openly. "Uncle Cory filled me in on how that rumor got its start. He was pushing the producer of his third movie to use *this* house in the film. Since the movie was about a gay ghost who liked to feel-up the male guests anytime a party was given, Uncle Cory started telling people that he lived in a house being haunted by a handsome male ghost."

"How utterly amusing." Raquel stares up at the ceiling rolling her eyes in frustration." No wonder my friends always tuned down Cory's invitations."

"Quit it. I, for one, think I will be very happy here. The house is beautiful. The furnishings are beautiful, and the grounds are beautiful."

"Would you at least promise me that you will always try to be home before dark? God only knows what could be running around out there through all those trees. And no, I am not talking about the deer and the chipmunks."

"Oh, come now. The only thing running around outside would be nothing more than a few Bigfoot's.

I hear the Pacific Northwest is very common for sightings." She tries to keep a straight face knowing her mother will believe anything frightening when it concerns the house and grounds.

"I hope if you do catch sight of him that you aren't dumb enough to invite him in. I would hate to be the grandmother of a bunch of little Bigfoots running around."

Her mother's quick wit had her laughing and drawing the older woman into her arms. "With your imagination, you should have been a writer."

"That's all right. I will leave the spotlight to you and Cory's memory. I had better take off. Your father wants to go out to dinner at that new restaurant in town, and you know how he gets when he is kept waiting a few moments. I would invite you to come along, but that would mean you would be getting back here after dark, and then I would be up all night pacing the floor worrying about you."

"No problem. I stocked the fridge and freezer. Uncle Cory had a lot of food in the freezer already, but since I had no idea how long it had been there, I gave it all to the food bank. Being frozen, I thought it would be all right for them to have."

"Okay, stay safe." She hugs Ronnie close before walking out the door.

In the car, Raquel stares out at the big house with the fancy windows and the backyard pool.

As she eyes the many acres of forest, she shutters, knowing there is no way she could ever live this far out in the wild. Turning the key, she backs the car out of the driveway, anxious to return to civilization where the only thing to fear in her gated community is a neighbor's crackhead son or daughter.

~*~

Ronnie walks upstairs to put the last of the clothes she had brought from her small apartment into a large dresser.

Sitting at the foot of the dual king-size bed, she laughs aloud as she thinks about her mother's suggestion for her to come back to live in their house again, after she has been moved out and on her own for the last nine years.

Thanks to her very lucrative career in modeling, she can be her own person and make her own decisions on what is important in her life. Right now, her top priority stems from finding a man to fall in love with, getting married, and being a mother to four or five kids to love and spoil. She had thought this would have all happened by now since she will be turning twenty-nine in the next few months. However, for some reason, she couldn't seem to find the right man. Either he was a user of women, too possessive, had no long-term plans to get anywhere in life, or he just did not turn her on. That was the biggest need to have. She wanted to feel something the moment she looked at him. There had to be that electric zing the moment their hands touched. Now, all she needs to do is find him.

Dressed now in a skimpy bikini she would never dare wear on a public beach, she drapes a thick towel over one shoulder to walk downstairs and out the sliding glass door to the Olympic-sized swimming pool.

Not willing to wait to test the temperature by sticking one toe in the water, she climbs up to the high diving board and, after inhaling a deep breath, dives into the water.

Her heart jumps in her throat as her distorted vision sees the image of someone standing by the side of the pool as she makes her way to the top.

"Sure hope I didn't frighten you. I was on my way here to take a swim, and I saw you dive into the water."

Ronnie swims to the end of the pool to walk up the blue-colored steps leading upward out of the pool.

"I'm Ronnie Westerlyne, the owner of this property. Who are you, and what are you doing here?"

"My name's Jason Talbert. Cory and I were close friends, and he said I could come for a swim anytime I wanted. I didn't know there was someone already moved in here."

Ronnie dries her face, wraps the thick towel

around her waist before pulling off the thin cap she wore to keep her hair dry.

Staring at the man standing in front of her, she admits to herself he is not the best-looking man she has ever come across, although he is not a bad-looking man with his mop of sandy hair brushing the collar of the shirt he is wearing above his prim swim trunks. She notices the way his dark blue eyes light up with interest as he gazes at her.

"So, do you mind if I take a swim since I'm already here?"

Ronnie grins, then nods as he pulls off his shirt and, without another word, dives headfirst into the water.

She stands where she is, watching him swim around the pool with easy strokes. She guesses his age to be in his late twenties-early thirties. She notices that although he doesn't have the muscular build of a man who works out, his tanned body shows he does take care of himself. She recalls how all her uncle's male friends were in good shape. A prerequisite, she gathered, to be a close friend of the famous Cory Williams.

She withdraws the small hair tie keeping her long hair tied back in a ponytail, then shakes her head, allowing the thick mane to cascade around her slender shoulders.

Ronnie walks inside to take a pitcher of

lemonade from the fridge and two tall glasses from the cupboard. Glancing out the window, she notices the absence of another car in the driveway.

"Guess he must have a cabin further back in the forest. Oh well, at least he isn't a Bigfoot," she murmurs to herself, laughing as she walks back out to the pool only to find her newly encountered visitor has already taken his leave.

CHAPTER TWO

"When you going to break down and go out with me, Ronnie? I'll make you smile." He turns up the collar of his light blue denim shirt, sticks one finger in a belt loop on his tight-fitting jeans to leer over at her.

"I wasn't aware you flipped back and forth, Dustin. Let me ask your latest conquest what he thinks about our going out on the town and get back to you."

"He'd be all for it as long as he can watch."

"Sorry, Dustin, but somehow you just don't fit into my choice of dating material." She laughs good-naturedly.

"Can't blame a handsome and spirited young dandy for trying. By the way, when are you going to throw one of those famous Cory parties out at your place? Surprised Cory didn't put it in the will that anyone who takes over his house has to throw one at least once or twice a month." He winks at her.

"I'll give that some thought."

"Remember, those parties were only for those proud of their package and smokin' hot bods. That went for all female partiers too. 'Course I can see you'd fit right in."

"Ready when you are, Ronnie," a girl in her early teens calls out.

Dustin picks up his camera as Ronnie strikes a pose. "All right, let's get that beautiful body on film so every man attracted to only women can thank the devil he's straight."

The woman in wardrobe places the expensive satin dress, Ronnie hands over to her, on a silk-wrapped coat hanger to place it with the rest of the clothing on the sturdy bar.

"Word has it, you're living in Cory's house. I gotta say while it's a gorgeous place, I couldn't live there. Too isolated for me. I'd be afraid something or someone would try and break in and kill me in the night."

Ronnie grins over at Thelma, the middle-aged, Auburn-haired woman dressed in baggy slacks and an oversized sweatshirt. "You sound like my mother. She is having fits that I am living there all alone, too."

"Could I ask you something, Ronnie, without you thinking I'm talking like a prude?"

"Sure."

"Did Cory throw nude pool parties at his place

like people say he did?"

"Knowing my uncle, there isn't anything I could think of that he wouldn't do if he took a notion to do it. And to hell with anyone who didn't like it."

"I probably shouldn't tell you this, you being his niece and all, but for a long time, I had a big crush on Cory. Even knowing he was gay. I always thought that all he needed was to meet the right woman, and she would change his sexual preferences. He was so handsome with that Auburn hair and those snapping green eyes." She wrapped her arms around her plump shoulders. "I used to daydream about what it would be like to be in his arms and...well... anyway," she glances up, a bright blush covering her face, "suffice it to say, I thought he was one hunk of a man."

"You and the millions of other men and women in the world. That and his talent for acting is what made him such a great star."

"Aren't you afraid to live in a house that is haunted? My stepbrother, Barry, used to go to Cory's parties. 'Course he wasn't into the gay scene," she hastened to add, "he was dating one of the women who helped the actresses with their lines. Anyway, when the weather was too cold for pool parties, Cory would sit with his guests in front of the big fireplace in the living room, sharing drinks and telling about all the strange things that went on in the house, especially at night."

"What kind of strange things?" Ronnie is beginning to feel a slight queasiness in the pit of her stomach since she always ignored all the gossip, being bantered about, on all the rumors.

"Barry said that Cory told them about a young man who liked to scare his guests, especially the ones who stayed after everyone else went home. If you get my drift," she laughed a nervous little giggle. "Guess he didn't approve of Cory's gay lifestyle."

"Maybe, but I would venture to guess that my uncle, being the great storyteller that he was, made it all up just to entertain his guests."

"You're probably right. Anyway, are you coming to the big party tonight, to celebrate Waldo Milestein's birthday? Never hurts to stay on the good side of a big film producer."

Ronnie zipped her jeans, pulled her t-shirt into place. "I haven't made up my mind yet. I have an early shoot tomorrow, so I will probably just skip the party and turn in early."

~*~

Pulling into the driveway, she puts the car in park and turns off the key. Grabbing the sack of fast food she picked up for dinner, she opens her car door to rush ahead of the rain that had started to fall.

Once inside, she drops the food on the island to rush into the nearest bathroom to grab a towel.

"Rain, rain scurry away," she sings aloud. "I

want to sit back and enjoy one of my classics this evening."

Seating herself on one of the stools pulled up to the island, she opens the fast food sack to remove the food when she hears the doorbell ring.

"Oh, Crap! I bet that's mom and dad here to talk me into going to the birthday party." She hops off the stool.

Pulling open the door, she is surprised to see the young man who had swum in the pool the day before.

"I hope I'm not interrupting anything. I was in the neighborhood and thought I would stop in to say hi." He grins a lopsided grin.

"Get in here out of the rain," she says, motioning him into the house. "I was just getting ready to eat my dinner. I will be glad to share some with you."

"No thanks. I already ate earlier."

"Okay, then can I offer you something to drink? I have sodas, hard liquor, and beer. You name it, I probably have it. Uncle Cory always kept a well-stocked bar."

"No, thanks. Go ahead and enjoy your dinner." He sits down on one of the stools.

"I notice you don't come and go in a vehicle, so I take it you live nearby?" She bites into her piece of chicken, chews then swallows.

"Yes, I live near here."

"What do you do for a living?"

"Until recently, I was a stuntman. That is how I met Cory. I was in the last three of his movies."

"I bet that can get pretty dangerous at times. I know Uncle Cory did a lot of his stunts, and they were hair-raising."

"That's the reason I was brought in. The producers said the movie backers were getting upset that Cory was risking his life on some of the stunts. Backers invest a lot of money in films. They don't want to take a chance on having a star as famous as Cory Williams kill himself."

"No kidding. Did you like being a stuntman, even though it was life-threatening sometimes?"

"Yes, I enjoyed it very much. The danger is what made the job so exciting." The grin covering his face made her smile.

"What made you quit if you enjoyed it so much?" She asked, going back to her food.

The grin disappears as he looks away. "I had a bad accident. Every bone in my body was broken. A crippled stuntman is of no use to the movie industry."

"But, look at you. You're fine now. I would think if you enjoyed what you did for a living that you would go back."

A somber look comes over his face, and he glances away. "Sometimes looks can be deceiving, Ronnie. At any rate, I best go on back home. I'm sure you have things you want to do."

"To tell you the truth, I would like you to stay if you have nothing planned." She swallows the last of her food. "Maybe by then, the rain will have let up. I hate to think of you returning to your place in a downpour. Why don't you stay here and keep me company? That is if you like classic movies. I will understand if the oldies aren't to your liking. Most people our age take a pass on them. I planned to watch my favorite this evening."

"I enjoy the classics very much." His enthusiasm tells her he is serious. "My favorite has always been Sayonara with Marlon Brando. Thanks."

"Sayonara has always been my favorite, too. And it is the one I have ready to watch tonight."

As the evening progresses, Ronnie is surprised and happy to see how they laugh at the same spots in the movie and nod at the same heart-warming line delivered by the smooth-talking cast.

When the movie ends, they continued to enjoy each other's company until the hour grows late.

"Wow. I didn't realize it is so late. I hate to bring this evening to an end, but I have an early shoot tomorrow. A model must look her best at all times, or the camera will tell the world she cheated on what time she turned in the night before."

"I enjoyed tonight, Ronnie. Maybe we can get together again sometime."

"I hope so, Jason. You are very easy to be with." She blushes, thinking she is being too flirtatious with someone she has just met the day before.

"I feel the same about you." He keeps his arms down to his side. "Good night." He turns, and without another word, he walks out the door leaving a smiling Ronnie wishing he didn't have to leave.

CHAPTER THREE

"How easy it would be to take you in my arms to hold you close if only for a moment. All my life, I searched for someone who could belong to only me. How sad that now when our lives can't intertwine, I find you."

Ronnie stretches out straight on her back, murmuring a low moan of contentment in her sleep.

"The moment I saw you, I knew I had to be near you. Not simply because of your gorgeous body, but to feel your energy, your spark of life, and to hear the musical sound of your beautiful voice. If only you could know how difficult it is to stand by your side without enjoying your touch. When the time is right, when we know each other better, I will not hold back on making my feelings known."

She sits up in bed and, swinging her legs off the side, gets to her feet to walk to the bathroom. Turning the faucet on cold, she cups a hand to catch the running water. After a few sips, she straightens up to look at herself in the mirror.

"What a strange dream. It was so real. Almost as though Jason was there. This is something I will keep to myself. If I were to share this with Mom, she would swear I have a dream lover."

On the ride to the studio, she thinks about Jason and admits to herself how much she enjoys being around him. He seemed to be an intelligent man. Someone who treated a woman with respect. He didn't even make a move to pull her close when getting ready to call it a night after they had spent the entire evening together. Most young men his age would have expected to receive a quick hug and a kiss on the cheek.

An unwelcome thought slam into her mind making her uneasy. Since he had been a close friend of her Uncle Cory, maybe the reason he isn't interested in being more than just a friend is that he isn't into women.

"Guess I'm not too quick on the uptake. He admitted to being a close friend of a man who was gay. He certainly looks the part of a man who would have caught Uncle Cory's attention. Why am I always on the outside looking in?" she murmurs to herself.

She pulls her light blue Jaguar into the studio's vast parking lot. At the same time, a red corvette parks in the space beside her.

Ronnie raises her hand in greeting as she gets out of the car.

"Guess we are both in for a long day," a beautiful blond-haired young woman says as she reaches out to give Ronnie a big hug.

"Good morning, Nicole. Yes, it would seem. Oh well, the money's right."

"You were missed at the big birthday bash for the all-important Milestein. You know he expects everyone he has ever allowed to do a scene in one of his movies to show up at any of his parties to fawn over him. Especially a personalized party such as his birthday."

"I'm surprised that he even realized I wasn't there with all the ass-kissing young starlets who were there."

"Trust me, they're kissing more than his ass. But, being the niece of the famous Cory Williams and Milestein's favorite star, your absence stuck out more than you realize."

"I'm sure he'll get over it."

"You need to get out more," Nichole tells her as they walk into the studio. "I bet you spent your evening alone eating fast food and watching one of your classic movies. I would die of complete boredom if that is all I did." She swings her head, tossing her long blond hair down her back.

"We should have put money on that bet because

you would have lost. While I did enjoy some fast food and watch one of my favorite movies, I wasn't alone."

"You have a cat or a dog. What kind did you get? No, don't tell me, let me guess. A Siamese or a German Shepherd."

"Neither, smartass. A man joined me. He is about my age, and he lives not too far from me. His name is Jason, and he is a cool guy."

"Is he good-looking? How is he in bed?" Nichole asked.

"I just met the man. While he is not movie-star good-looking, he's not bad. He was a good friend of my Uncle Cory."

"Wait." Nichole pulls her to a stop. "He was a good friend of your Uncle Cory? The Uncle Cory who was gay and threw nude pool parties at his estate?"

"Nichole, not everyone who went to the parties was gay. That is unless you aren't telling me something."

"Very funny, Ronnie." She grins over at her. "I went to give Cory a chance to get a good look at me in a bikini and ask me to be in one of his movies." She struck a pose. "Let's face it. I'm a gold-digging user bitch."

"I don't blame you for trying to get ahead. To tell you the truth, the thought about Jason being one of Uncle Cory's friends has crossed my mind, too. I hope he isn't gay. I think he and I could get close."

"I hope you get it worked out. Right now, it's time to go to work so we can afford to buy what we need to keep looking like we do."

"Later, Nichole." Ronnie waves her off.

"Missed you last night," Dustin said, coming forward. "And believe me when I say, I was not the only one. I heard the birthday boy telling your mom and dad that he thought it very disrespectful of you not to show up at his birthday bash."

"He'll live. I couldn't care less if he wants me to be in one of his movies again. I earn a good living, and I am happy with how my life already is."

"Spend one night with me, and I guarantee you, you'll be a lot happier." Dustin gives her shoulder a light squeeze.

"Dustin, have you heard about all the news reports on sexual harassment? If all the girls here were to make a complaint on your *less than respectful* actions, your job would be in the toilet."

Dustin breaks out in a flurry of laughter. "Ronnie, that surly attitude is makin' my point. After one night with me, you would be so relaxed and happy you would be beggin' me to move in with you."

"No thanks, Dustin, I already have a real man who takes care of my needs," she lies.

Dustin looks at her for a moment then turns to get busy with his equipment.

"Great, I just told the biggest loudmouth here

that I am in a relationship. Now all I'll hear is a lot of nosey questions about my love life. Or more to the point, my nonexistent love life," she murmurs.

Ronnie pulls the soft sweater she was wearing over her head, then reaches for her phone lying on the small shelf in the dressing room.

"Let me take that sweater," Thelma tells her, removing the sweater from her hands.

"Hello," Ronnie answers the call.

"Hi, Hon, it's Mom. Are you busy at the moment?"

"Hold on a moment," she says, pulling a shirt on before walking out of the dressing room. "Okay, what's up?"

"Mr. Milestein was upset that you didn't come to his party. Ronnie, you know that to climb the success ladder, you have to do things you don't like sometimes."

"I am well aware that if I want to be in movies again, I am expected to kiss Milestein's ass. Since I could give a flip less if I am in another movie, I was completely content to stay home and enjoy myself."

"I think you are making a big mistake."

"If Milestein is so needy, then why the hell doesn't he move out to Hollywood and be with all the rest of the losers? One would think that since he lives here in the Pacific Northwest, he is above all the hoopla."

"I agree, but I guess he isn't. Listen. Your father and I would like to join you for dinner this evening. This way, you will be home, and safe inside after the sun goes down. We will bring dinner. Since we are inviting ourselves, I think this is the least we can do."

"You know you and Dad are always welcome. What time will you be coming over?"

"7:ish or thereabout. See you then."

"Yes, see you." She turns off the phone, drops it in her purse. She buttons the shirt then, slinging the purse strap over her shoulder, walks from the dressing room.

"Didn't mean to eavesdrop on your conversation," Dustin says, coming forward. "Sounds like the parents are going to be coming over."

"Yes. I always enjoy visiting with them."

"I take it you will be including your new love in the family feast."

"Oh yes. I am sure I will. Never too early for the in-laws to meet their future son-in-law." She turns before Dustin can see the satisfied grin covering her face at his sour look.

~*~

On her way home, Ronnie drives around, trying to see a place set back in the trees near her property. After an hour of searching, she has to admit defeat.

"Where in the hell could he be living? Since he doesn't arrive in a vehicle, that means he has to walk to get anywhere."

Noticing the time, she heads home to jump in the shower and get ready for her parents' arrival.

She puts the finishing touch on her makeup just as the doorbell rings, announcing their arrival. Racing down the stairs, she opens the door then stands back, allowing them to come in.

"Knowing you keep your door locked makes me happy. No sense taking chances," Raquel says, walking past her on her way to the kitchen.

"You could have an armed guard surrounding this place, and she would still whine that you aren't safe here," her father tells her, running a hand through his thick black hair.

Ronnie eyes her father's dark green shirt and black slacks before pulling him close to place a loud kiss on his freshly shaved cheek. "You always smell so good, Dad."

"Ronnie, if you will set the table, we can be seated. Jim, I'll let you pour the wine."

When all was ready, they began to dine on the flavorful food Raquel had purchased for them from her favorite Italian restaurant.

"So, tell me all about the party last night. I know you are dying to fill me in."

"It was a star-studded bash like always. Many big stars flew in to be there. I can't believe you didn't go."

"I can. Our daughter has some common sense," Jim says, forking up a bit of his salad.

"She also has a career to think about."

"I already have a great career that earns me good money, and I am happy to leave it at that."

"Ronnie, with your looks, you could be a big star, just as your Uncle Cory was," Raquel tells her, running a hand over her silver-colored silk dress to brush away a few crumbs from a piece of toasted Italian bread.

"I'll pass," she said, taking a large drink of her wine. "I want to meet a nice guy who likes the same things I do. A man who wants to be the father of at least four, maybe five kids. That is my idea of happiness."

"What are some of the same things you would want him to like?" Jim asks, glancing at her.

"I would like him to be able to enjoy staying home to watch some of the old classics with me instead of going to parties where everything said has to be predicated on being politically correct."

"Here, here." Jim laughs, holding his wine glass high.

"In other words, you want a man just like dear old dad," her mother says, a slight giggle sounding in her tone of voice.

"I would say that pretty well sums it up, Mama."

CHAPTER FOUR

Knowing she cannot wait any longer for Jason to pay her another visit, she gives up as she begins turning off lights in the big house.

As always, she leaves a small lamp burning in the living room. This way, the house is never in total darkness. Somehow, knowing this makes her feel better.

Ronnie laughs aloud, thinking how afraid she had always been when hearing spooky stories, even though Halloween was one of her favorite holidays. She loved to dress up in her favorite costume and go out with the children of her parents' friends.

Now, here she is, living in a large house surrounded by acres of forest, and she isn't afraid. It is almost as though she doesn't live in the house alone. Even so, she doesn't like to dwell on the fact that she does live in the big house alone. That if danger should find her, no one could reach her in time to save her.

In the bathroom, she removes her makeup before pulling a flimsy nightgown over her head to pull it into place.

"If I ever do find my lasting love, he won't have anything to bitch about with my choice of lingerie." She gazes at herself in the long mirror, liking what she sees.

"I can't believe how some of the girls at the studio say they don't want children because it will ruin their figure. I can't wait until I have a child growing beneath my heart."

She clicks off the light and walks into the large bedroom to turn down the covers on the bed.

"I wonder if Jason will come and be my dream lover again tonight. I'm almost tempted to tell him about how he played a part in an exciting few moments of my slumber. But, he's so prim and proper he might take offense."

She stretches out in the middle of the bed, places an arm over her forehead.

"I hope his prim and proper ways don't mean what I think it might."

She sits up as a thought slams into her mind. "Enough of these silly what-ifs. The next time we meet, I am going to ask him straight out if he is straight or gay. I have wasted enough time looking for a man I can call my own. If it turns out he *is* gay, then I will simply treat him as I would any other of my female friends. However, if it turns out he is straight, I'm going to jump him."

With that said, she stretches her body out straight and, within moments, falls into a relaxing sleep.

Jason sits down beside her on the large bed, and reaching out, he runs one hand over the side of her face.

Ronnie smiles, feeling gentle energy flowing easily throughout her body.

"Why have you waited so long to come into my life?" she whispers in her sleep. "I want you to be the man I will never wish to lose. The man who will be the father of my children."

"Hear me and remember my words, Ronnie. I can only offer you these stolen moments. I can never be the father of your children or the husband you have long searched for. Too I can only hold you close if you say it is all right. I have remained on this plane for selfish reasons, but there will come a time when I will return home, and I want my soul to be welcome. There are rules on the other side that must not be broken.

"If this is all you can offer, then I will have to be content with what you can give me. I only know I have to have you in my world. Stay with me, Jason."

Jason stands to disrobe, gazing all the while at the beautiful woman sleeping peacefully. He lifts the covers, then stretches out on the bed to draw Ronnie into his arms.

Her body responds to his touch, and she snuggles up to him.

Holding her close in his arms, tears at his heart. Of all the women he had been in his young life, the woman lying next to him is the one to make him feel the most wanted.

All through the night, they remain in each other's arms. Early the next morning, she remains very still, wanting to hold onto their moments together as long as she can. Then with a groan, she gets to her feet.

"What a strange and beautiful dream."

She pads to the bathroom, thinking all the while about the man she has just enjoyed being with.

On her way back, she glances at the clock noting she still has a few hours before she has to get up. Climbing back into bed, she turns over on her side to fall back into a deep and comforting sleep.

Jason stands by the bed watching her, and he feels his heart ache with sadness. "I know it is time for me to go home. I am only prolonging what I have to do. I also know I should not have given into my weakness and held you all through the night, for now, my walking away is even more difficult than before I met you. You deserve to find a man who can give you all you need in this life. To give you all that

I am unable to give you while I dwell on this plane. This dark place we leave home to visit and learn life's lessons. What have I done to deserve such a cruel and heartless joke?" Anger enters his voice, and he does nothing to quiet it.

"I have searched all my life for the right woman only to find her after my spirit has left my body. My heart that is no longer of the flesh still aches, and my loins still hunger to be satisfied. But, I know that while my spirit lives in this empty shell, I can do nothing to satisfy *my* needs. It is too late for me to know the joy of having *my* own family, and I don't think I am strong enough to see you in the arms of another." His spirit begins to fade as he turns away.

"Please, don't walk away from what we have found," Ronnie murmurs in her sleep.

Upon hearing her quiet words, Jason turns back to walk over to the bed. "While I won't be able to stay long, I will wait to return home." He leans down and places a soft kiss on the side of her face. "Rest now, my beautiful Ronnie, and know that we will be together again."

Ronnie caresses the place his lips have touched, and she smiles.

She carries a smile all through that day, and each time she catches Dustin looking at her, the smile grows until it covers her face.

"Looks like last night was a real winner. You're

all but dancin' on the ceiling."

"Oh yes, last night was a night to remember."

"So, what do Mom and Dad think of your new love?"

They didn't get a chance to meet him last night. They left before he came over."

"Then why all the glowing smiles?" The look on his face as he gazes at her is one of complete bafflement.

Ronnie looks at him, then bursts out laughing. "And I thought you a savvy guy."

CHAPTER FIVE

Forking up a bit of her tossed salad with slices of chicken across the top, she puts the food into her waiting mouth when she hears the doorbell ring.

Hopping off the stool, she goes to answer the door. "I sure hope this is who I think it is."

Smiling, she pulls open the door only to find herself staring into the gross and repugnant face of Waldo Milestein.

"Mr. Milestein. This is a surprise," she stammers.

"Please, Ronnie, call me Waldo. I have a feeling you and I are going to be close friends." He laughs as he spreads his hands wide. "Are you going to invite me in?"

Ronnie feels her stomach tighten as she steps to the side to let him come into the house.

"Why don't we go sit down, and you can offer me something to drink. I could always depend on Cory to have a well-stocked bar. My pleasure, or at least one of them," he snorts a throaty laugh, "is a triple shot of your best scotch. No ice."

"Of course, have a seat, and I will fix you a drink." She gestures to one of the stools surrounding the island.

"Oh, I think we can do better than a stool in the kitchen. I was thinking more like in the living room on the couch." His voice is low as his pale blue eyes flow slowly over her slender figure.

Nodding, Ronnie makes her way over to the bar to remove one of the many glasses lined up on a shelf. Lifting an almost full bottle of what she knows to be a very expensive brand of scotch, she pours a liberal amount into a glass.

"You're not only very beautiful, but now I can see you are also a very good hostess. A wealthy man would do well to have you for a wife."

"To what do I owe this visit?" She seats herself in a chair facing the couch.

"Only the best for Cory Williams." He grins over at her, lifting his glass in the air before taking a drink. "Aren't you going to join me in a drink? I hear it's never good for a person to drink alone. Gives them a bad rep."

"No, I'll pass. You haven't answered my question on what brings you, *unannounced*, to my home, Mr. Milestein." Her tone of voice is straight and to the point.

"All right, I guess it is a little early for you to be informal and call me by my first name. So, for now, I will accept that."

Ronnie remains silent, watching him.

"The reason I am here is to tell you that I might have a part in my upcoming film that you would be right for. You certainly have the looks for the part, and as you have already proven you can act, I am going to give you a chance to see yourself on the big screen again. Your mother asked me to talk with you about it, and I agreed. Raquel is very much into the movie scene and would be very happy to see her little girl climb the success ladder and be a star just as her brother Cory was."

"Thank you, Mr. Milestein, but I already have a very lucrative career that keeps me quite busy. Sorry, you had to drive out here for nothing."

"You are not serious." He draws back, staring at her. "I am a very important man in this business, and you have the *unmitigated* nerve to turn down an offer that could make you a star!" He gets to his feet. "You are choosing to be an unknown willing to take off her clothes if a magazine calls for it while I am here offering you a part in a big film, and you turn me down!"

Ronnie gets uneasily to her feet. "I think we have said all there is to say, Mr. Milestein. It is time you are on your way."

Without a word, he walks over to the bar and, picking up the bottle of scotch, refills his glass. He looks at her, then throws the liquor down his throat.

"If you think I am leaving here without getting what I came here to get, you are very wrong, little girl. I have had my eye on you for quite some time now, and I feel I have waited long enough."

"You are too full of yourself," Ronnie tells him. Her voice cold with the disgust she is feeling.

"No one turns down Waldo Milestein. Do you hear me, missy?! No one! Either you do as you're told, or that modeling career you are so proud of will be over."

"Oh really?" She looks him right in his eyes. "And just what do you think your name will be like after I let it be known all over tinsel town that the ugly, obese, and baldheaded Waldo Milestein can only get a woman on her back by using threats?"

For a fleeting instant, she sees fear leap into his watery blue eyes. Then, it is gone as he gives her a smug grin.

"Have you looked around you lately, Ronnie? Have you forgotten that you live alone in the middle of 100-acres of forest? No one will hear your screams for help. And if worse comes to worst, no one will even find your body."

"Are you threatening me, Milestein?" She allows the anger to boil forth at the thought of this ugly and filthy man reeking of rolls of fat the air cannot get to try to coerce her into allowing him to have sex with her. "Are you saying that either I let you have sex with me and keep quiet about it, or you are going to kill me?"

"You have a lot of spunk. I like that in a woman; makes them more of a challenge." He licks his lips as he walks towards her.

"You need to think about your status in the film business and leave, Milestein. You're not going to cower me into doing what you want. I am the niece of the famous Cory Williams, and I have as much clout, if not more, in the movie business as you do."

"You filthy little bitch! Do you dare to threaten me? Get your clothes off right now! Get them off!"

The pure hatred covering his hideous face pushes her to turn and run to the front door.

"You stupid bitch! There is nowhere for you to run," he screams at her as he moves quickly to block her escape.

"Don't you dare put your filthy fat hands on me. I would rather die right here in my own home than let you smother me with your reeking fat body."

The loud chiming of the doorbell makes them both stop.

"Shut up!" He hisses a warning, yanking her backward to cover her mouth. "You will shut the hell up and let them think you aren't home. If you utter one word, I will break your filthy neck!"

Ronnie reaches back her hand, grabs onto Milestein's crouch, and squeezes, making him scream and remove his hands. Before he has a chance to stop her, she runs screaming to yank open the front door.

At the sight of Jason standing in the open doorway, Ronnie falls sobbing into his arms.

Without a word, Jason pulls her close to gaze over her shoulder at the man glaring at them with extreme anger.

Milestein shakes his head, then rubs his eyes for a moment before bringing his gaze back to the man smiling at him as he holds Ronnie protectively in his arms.

The two people still standing in the open doorway hear a long and drawn-out moan, then a loud thud as, who only scant moments earlier was making serious threats on her life, falls over onto the floor.

Ronnie jerks around, and at seeing Milestein on the floor, his eyes open and bulging with horror, she moves over to him and, bending down, places her fingertips against his neck.

A satisfied laugh escapes her throat as she looks up at Jason. "His fat ass won't be raping and threatening young starlets anymore."

Getting to her feet, she walks over to pick up her cell phone.

As the call picks up, she tells the person on the other line to send an ambulance for a person whom she believes has had a massive heart attack and is no longer alive. After she gives them her address, she turns off the phone to lay it back down on the island.

"You can bet this is going to make the headlines," she tells Jason as they walk around the body to go into the living room.

Without stopping to think about what she was going to do, Ronnie turns and places a kiss on Jason's cheek.

"Thank you for showing up when you did. When he saw I was not going to stop fighting him and let him rape me, he went completely crazy with anger. I believe he would have followed through on killing me. Now I know what all those poor young girls and women he did rape felt like. Waldo Milestein was a very evil man. Much too evil to hold that much power over the lives of others."

"I'm just glad I chose this time to stop by. I had the misfortune to run into Milestein a few times on different movie sets I was hired to do stunts on. He always struck me as a person who would go to any lengths to get what he wanted, no matter who he had to hurt. He didn't only go after little girls and young women, he would also go after young men, and their age didn't matter. Someone that bent on the destruction of others does not deserve to live."

Ronnie looks at him for a long moment then goes ahead with what she wants to ask.

"Did he come onto you, Jason?"

"He tried. He told me he would see to it that I never got another stunt job if I refused him. He backed off real fast when I threw a fist into his face and told him I would go to the press with what he was threatening to do and also talk about the other young men and girls he was coming onto."

"Good for you. I'm glad his last moments on earth were filled with pain. I used the martial arts I took a class in on what a woman can do if she is ever threatened with bodily harm, especially rape. Guess his heart attack was brought on by his extreme pain."

"Yeah, that and the shock he got at seeing me standing in the doorway."

CHAPTER SIX

"Ronnie!" a young woman calls out over the loud clamor of clicking cameras. "Can you tell us what Waldo Milestein came out here to talk with you about?"

Ronnie smiles for the camera as a young man from her favorite news affiliation reaches a microphone out to her.

"He came out to offer me a part in a film he was getting ready to shoot. I declined his offer," she told them.

"Waldo Milestein was very big in the film industry. He could have made you a star. Why did you turn him down on his offer?" The young man gives her a puzzled look.

"He was asking too big a price for the part." Ronnie gazes over at him.

"Yes, there are a lot of rumors floating around about his dalliances with young starlets," a woman from another news affiliate said, her voice filled with doubt. "Course, now that he is no longer here to defend himself, I guess we can only chalk up the rumors to hearsay."

"If I were you, I would stick close to the Waldo Milestein death story. I have a feeling that a lot of young women and young men will be coming out of the woodwork to talk about their unhappy run-ins with the movie mogul now that he can no longer influence their careers." She smiles a challenging smile as the woman lowers her mike and turns away.

As the news people put away their equipment, Ronnie and her mother walk into the house.

Raquel sets down on one of the stools and drops her purse on the island. "I can't tell you how sorry I am for talking Waldo Milestein into coming to talk with you about a movie part. However, I had no idea he had a bad heart. I guess I should have since a man his size could not have been in the best of health. When you called to tell me what happened, I was stunned."

Ronnie hugs her mother close to her for a moment before stepping back to walk over to the fridge. "I'm going to have a glass of OJ. Would you care for a glass, or would you rather I get you something a little stronger?"

"Juice will be fine. Thanks. What was all that you were talking about concerning Milestein and young people? Were you hinting that he was coming onto them?"

"I was not hinting. Waldo Milestein was a monster. A monster that deserves to burn in hell for the terrible harm he has done to countless young women and men who only wanted to get on with their careers." She sets down their glasses of juice before pulling out the stool closest to the one her mother is sitting on.

"Ronnie, how do you know this is true?" Raquel draws back her head to look at her. "If this is only conjectured on your part, his family can sue you for defamation of character, and I would not blame them. He was a big name in Hollywood." She takes a sip of her juice.

"I know this is true because he came here to dangle a part in a film, making it quite clear that all I had to do is have sex with his fat ass. When I declined his generous offer, he threatened to ruin my modeling career. Only he didn't stop there. When I still refused him, he threatened to kill me."

"Oh my god! I had no idea." She turned on the stool to stare over at her. "Oh, Ronnie. I am so sorry. I would never have asked him to come and visit you had I had any inkling of how sick and twisted he was."

"I know this, Mama. If Jason hadn't arrived when he did, I don't think I would be alive."

"Yes, tell me about this, Jason. You said he lives

around here, and you only met him a few days ago."
She finishes the last of her glass of juice.

"That's right, I met him the same day you came
over trying to talk me into moving back with you and
Dad. He showed up for a swim soon after you left.
He's a good person. He stayed with me yesterday
long after the police and the ambulance took Milestein
away. I guess he and Uncle Cory were close friends,
and he used the pool a lot."

"If he was close friends with Cory, he is
probably gay."

"I don't think so. I thought the same thing at
first, but when he told me about Milestein coming
onto *him* and how he had punched him in the face, I'm
inclined to think he's straight." She laughs. "Not only
that, but Milestein had the nerve to threaten Jason's
career as a stunt man. Jason was in a few of Uncle
Cory's films. I think that is how they met."

"I will have to meet this new friend of yours
and thank him for coming to the aide of my daughter.
Is he a young man or older?"

"He's about my age. Not a handsome man, but
each time I see him, he seems to get better looking. I
think the reason for my seeing him in a different light
is because I see his wholesome side, and this makes
me look at him differently. He had a terrible accident
during one of his stunts. It would be my guess he is
on disability, although you would never know it to

look at him."

"Sounds as though you and this young man hit it off." Raquel smiles.

"We find we have a few things in common. He enjoys watching the classics, and believe it or not, his favorite movie is the same as mine."

"Has he made a move yet?" She had to laugh when she saw the slight grin that played at the corners of Ronnie's full mouth.

"Truth be told, he hasn't even given me a good night hug or a peck on the cheek."

"He sounds like a very respectful young man. You never know. This could turn into something. I know how much you want to find a man to settle down with and start a family."

"Yep. Not getting any younger. I am sure you and Dad would like to have some grandkids to hold in your arms and spoil."

"Yes, we would, and speaking of your dad, I am going to go on home and fill him in on what all happened. He should be back home by now. He had to go out of town on business. I just hope I can beat the news. The death of Waldo Milestein will be on all the stations. You can bet on that."

"Too bad they don't have a TV in hell. You can bet he would want to be in the center of everything those in Hollywood will have to say about him."

"I know one thing for sure. Milestein can thank

his lucky stars that your father didn't have the chance to get ahold of him. You are his pride and joy, and to know that something as sick as Milestein tried to put his filthy hands on you would not have ended well."

"Makes me feel special to know I have a dad who loves me so much."

"Getting back to your young man, I would like to have the two of you over for dinner some night. I would love to meet him, and I know your father will want to shake his hand."

"All right. The next time Jason stops by, I will see what he thinks of the idea."

As her mother drives off down the lane, Ronnie closes the door to stand quietly for a moment. Then, she walks over to the bar. Taking a glass from the shelf, she fills it partway full with some orange-laced Vodka. With a drink in hand, she walks into the front room to seat herself in her uncle's favorite recliner.

"Sure could use your comfort right now, Uncle Corey. I always believed that nothing bad could ever happen to me if you or Dad were nearby. Guess I was proven right because while neither of you was here, the devil showed up and thought, since I'm all alone, he could do whatever he wanted. He found out he was wrong. It's almost like you left someone to protect me since you can no longer be here. If this is true, then I thank you for loaning me your good friend Jason. He's turning out to be not only my Godsend," she giggles quietly, "but believe it or not, my dream lover."

CHAPTER SEVEN

Snuggled beneath the covers, Jason cups her face with both hands to place a sweet and loving kiss on her open mouth.

"You are safe, my Ronnie," he tells her as he leans over her. "As long as I continue to dwell on this plane and in this house, I will protect you from all harm."

"You are my Godsend, Jason. The one I know I can count on to come to my aid," she whispers in her slumber. "You remind me of my Uncle Cory." She smiles. "He always stayed close to me when I was visiting with him here."

"There is so much I wish I could share with you, but I am not sure this is the time. I don't want to frighten you away since we've only known each other for such a short time."

"I don't think you can frighten me away unless my saying that I think I am falling in love with you would frighten you away."

Jason sits up on the side of the bed. "My beautiful Ronnie, I fear I have done you a terrible injustice. I am not the man you need in your life, for I cannot remain in your life. You said you want a husband and children. I cannot fulfill either of those needs. I think it would be better if I were to leave and let you find this man you want." He gets up from the bed to stand, staring down at her, unable to stop the pain her words have given him.

"Please don't go, Jason. I feel you are more than just my dream lover. You must not be afraid to tell me what you feel I need to know."

"If only I could be sure you would not run away after learning the truth of my visits. In the beginning, I only came to see if you were doing all right, at the request of a friend, then, after I was with you, I knew you were someone I never wanted to leave. As much as you want me to stay and as much as I want to stay, I'm afraid we have broken each other's hearts." With that being said, he turned and walked out of the room to leave a saddened Ronnie crying quietly in her sleep.

~*~

All that day, Ronnie found herself besieged by people wanting to know what had happened to bring on Milestein's untimely death while he was visiting her home. While she didn't like being rude, at the same time, all she wanted to do was be by herself to remember the words still so clear in her mind that Jason said to her in last night's dream.

"Ronnie, are you the talk of the town or what?" Dustin said as he removes a backdrop to replace it with a picture of the sea.

"As much as I don't want to be, I guess I am," she tells him, adjusting the flimsy bikini bra to a more comfortable position.

"I hear he offered you a part in his upcoming film, and you turned him down. That had to be a real blow to the ego. Two things he isn't used to being refused of; a blow *and* the offer of a movie role, all in one setting." Dustin laughs aloud. "Why the hell did you turn him down? You could be right up there with Cory in a year or two."

"Milestein had nothing I wanted. He was a fat pig who thought he owned Hollywood and every male or female who had the misfortune to cross his path."

"Wow." Dustin stood up. "I swear, the more I see of you, and the more I hear about how you stayed off Milestein, I thank my lucky stars that I am at least bi and not of the female charts."

"Save it, Dustin. I already told you that you aren't my type. Besides, if your boyfriend hears you coming onto me, you're apt to get a fist in your face and more than what you're used to up your ass!"

"Stop! You're turning me on!" he cried, holding

the backdrop in front of his crotch as he spied a man
he recognized walking towards them. "I think you're
about to have a mike shoved in your face. He's one of
those losers who should be working on a fake news
station."

"I don't want to take up much of your time as
I can see you are busy, so let me introduce myself,
and we can get on with hearing a few words for our
listening audience." He held the mike in front of his
face. "My name is Samuel Jones. What can you tell us
that has not already been told in the news of why you
were entertaining Mr. Milestein in your home miles
away from civilization?"

Ronnie pulls loose a towel draped over the back
of a chair to tie it around her waist. "As you can see, I
am working, so you need to be on your way."

"I am working too, and I am trying to get a
story from you. You're big news right now, and if
you're smart, you will enjoy your 15-minutes of fame
while you can." His condescending voice rises with
his anger.

Dustin put a restraining arm in front of Ronnie.
"I'll handle this," he tells her. "You've been told we're
working here, so you would be smart to be on your
way. Miss Westerlyne already made it clear that she
has nothing to say to you. Not now, not ever, so the
best thing you can do is leave."

"You dare to use that tone of voice with me? I

am Samuel Jones! If you bothered to watch the news, you would know I am one of the most popular news reporters in the world! I flew all the way here from New York just to get a story from you. Now again, why was Waldo Milestein visiting you at your home, and what were the two of you dallying in, at the precise moment, to bring on his massive heart attack?"

"I have this, Dustin," she says, putting out her hand as Dustin starts coming forward. "I have nothing to say to you, Jones. Furthermore, if you keep bothering me, I will be forced to call your news station and tell them you are harassing me. And if that isn't enough to get your skinny ass out of here, I will let all the big news stations know that before Milestein dropped dead, he let me know that you are one of the lousiest pieces of ass he ever wasted his time bending over a director's chair."

Immediately, a red-faced Jones places his mike back inside a small carrying case and, turning away, makes a speedy retreat out of the studio.

"Did Milestein tell you that, or were you just trying to piss off Jones enough to leave, which, as we can see, worked its magic."

"I'll keep that piece of info to myself." Ronnie smiles up at him. Then in a surprise move, she reaches out her arms to give Dustin a big hug. "Thank you for standing up to that non-talented trash."

"No problem." He pulls her close for a brief

moment. "I don't like bullies."

"That makes two of us."

"If I promise not to breathe a word of it to anyone else, can you trust me enough to tell me what happened to Milestein? I mean, what brought on his heart attack?" Granted, the piece of puke was about a good 350lbs. overweight, but what caused it to come on right then?"

"I refused to have sex with him after he was nice enough to offer me a role in his new film, which I declined. He got so mad at being turned down, he threatened to kill me."

"Are you serious?" Dustin's eyes widened with shock. "That ugly tub of lard threatened to kill you? What a piece of shit!"

"He said that since I lived out in the woods, no one would ever find my body."

"How did you get away from him?"

"One of Uncle Cory's friends showed up ringing the doorbell. I grabbed Milestein in the crotch to make him turn me loose and ran to yank open the door and fall into the arms of whoever was there. I guess Milestein was so angry at not getting his way that it brought on a massive heart attack."

"What in the world possessed one of Cory's friends to show up at that time? Everyone knows Cory doesn't live there anymore."

"Jason used to come over and use the pool a lot.

He still is. This is how we met. I guess he was not only a good friend of Uncle Cory but also a stuntman in a few of his films."

"Yeah, I've met Jason. However, you can't be talking about the same Jason who worked in Cory's films. That Jason died a short time back from a bad accident in one of his stunts. Guess he broke every bone in his body. Hell of a nice guy and a top-of-the-line stuntman. Everyone felt bad when he died."

"No, we can't be talking about the same man," Ronnie whispers, turning away.

"I think we can wrap it up for the day, Ronnie. See you in the morning. Be here early as we're going to be shooting at the beach. With that loser Jones taking up so much time, we got behind. Therefore, instead of doing a shoot here with the backdrop, we'll shoot it at the beach. We can all ride out there together. This means I'll get to enjoy seeing you in one of your hot bikinis again."

"Yeah," she said, walking towards the dressing room.

She only wanted to go home, to try to sort out in her mind what Dustin had told her.

CHAPTER EIGHT

As she drove, her mind stayed on Jason. "This has to be some kind of mistake. Why would the man I know as Jason Talbert lie to me and take another man's name?" The thoughts flipped nonstop through her mind.

"Then too, why can't I find where he is supposed to live further back in the woods? Why is there never a vehicle in the driveway when he shows up? And why does he always refuse to join me for dinner or even a drink?"

Turning into the driveway, she put the car in park, then turned off the key.

On her way to the door, a loud chirp breaks the silence as she clicks on the car alarm.

Walking into the house, she heads straight for the bar to take down a tall glass. Uncapping a bottle of OJ-laced Vodka, she pours a liberal amount into the glass. Dropping cubes of ice into her drink, she heads to the front room to plop down in the recliner.

"All right, Jason or whatever your name is, I want to know what the hell is going on. Are you only a figment of my imagination, or are you a ghost? Are you a real man or a spirit who enters my dreams at night? Either I am going nuts, or someone is here. *Have* I been entertaining a ghost?"

Lifting the glass to her mouth, she drinks until she feels her throat burn from the liquor. Reaching over, she sets the glass down on an end table beside the recliner.

"Ronnie, are you ready to hear the truth?"

She jerks around to see Jason standing across the room.

"How did you get in the house? Did Uncle Cory leave a key with you?"

She knows her voice and her face have to be showing him how uneasy he is making her feel, but she is unable to help herself.

"No, Ronnie, he didn't. But then I don't need a key to come and go from this house."

"You are frightening me, Jason." She sat forward in her chair. "I thought we were friends," she whispers.

"I don't mean to scare you, and yes, we are friends. But I believe the time has come for you to know the truth about me and what I am doing here."

"Is your name Jason Talbert and are you the

Jason Talbert who was killed a short time back as I have been told?"

"Before I answer all the questions I know you must have, can I come and sit near you?"

When she nodded, he moved a footstool over near the recliner.

Jason reached out, taking her hand in his. When she doesn't pull away, her apparent trust earns her a broad smile.

"All right, you deserve to know the truth. First, I want you to know I will never physically harm you."

Not willing to waste any more time, Ronnie repeated her question. "Is your name Jason Talbert and are you the Jason Talbert I have been told was killed recently?" She watches as different expressions cross his face.

"Yes."

Ronnie drew back her hand, starting to rise from her chair.

"Please hear me out. In the short time we have known one another, have I ever given you a reason to fear being alone with me?"

"No." She sits back down in her chair to lift the glass from the end table.

"That is right, and I never will. When I told you about my injuries in that stunt accident, I deliberately omitted the fact that I also died in that accident."

"Why did you not tell me the truth?"

"I knew if I told you about my death, you would run away from me in fear. I wanted to be near you a while longer. It was wrong of me to be so selfish."

"How were you able to come into my dreams?"

"When the mind is relaxed in slumber, that is when most people have a visit from a loved one who has left their body to go home to the other side, or like me, stay here for a while longer. The one receiving the visit believes they are only *dreaming* of a lost love, but when a visit is very vivid, it is not a dream. Someone is there with you."

"I always thought a ghost was only vapor; that they could not be touched or be held in someone's arms as a living person can.

"Do you want to hear something that is going to sound very strange to you? Until I found you, I was so cold, even standoffish." He looks away from her. "I didn't want others around me. I didn't have time to listen to their silly prattle. I was so unfeeling I might as well have been dead. When I had sex with a woman, I paid for that sex. I didn't want any strings attaching me to someone. I didn't want kids." Then without warning, his voice deepened to a more loving tone. "Now, for the first time, I find myself wanting to be with someone. I wait for you to come home each evening and at night; I can't wait to hold you in my arms. When you told me how you longed to get married and have children, I suddenly found myself wanting the same thing. I have never felt more alive."

"I have never felt more alive, either." She relaxes back in her chair.

"To answer your question about what a ghost can do, *they* allow who can and can't see them. There is no reason to eat or drink, as they no longer need to keep their body healthy. However, if we want to eat and drink something, we can, and those on the other side often do."

"I told my mother about you, and she wants the two of us to come to dinner some night so she and my father can meet the man who saved their daughter from being killed by Milestein."

"I am afraid I will have to decline her kind offer as it is not easy for me to keep a substance for very long. My spirit dwells in the empty shell you see before you. Also, there are pictures of me when I was a stunt man, and my obituary is complete with my picture. You would not want your parents to see me, thinking I am a living, breathing man then, see pictures of me and a story talking about my death."

"That's all right. I will make up some story of why you don't want to meet them."

"Believe me, it isn't that I don't want to meet your parents and spend time with all of you together. I'm sorry to be so much trouble. If we were honest with each other, we would agree that it would be better for both of us if I was to cross over and if you were to meet a man who can give you the family you so desperately want."

"I want you." She holds out her arms to him.

He left the footstool to pull her into his arms. "We are only prolonging our pain when we must say goodbye, but right now, all I want to do is hold you."

"You saved my life when you kept Milestein from raping and killing me because I do not doubt in my mind he meant to do both."

"I will never allow anyone to harm you if I can prevent it."

"I'm glad he is dead."

"I do have to laugh when I think about the look of terror crossing his face when he saw me. He came to my funeral so he could not pretend he was not seeing a ghost."

"That could shock anyone into having a heart attack, even someone who isn't obese."

"Waldo Milestein was a very evil and foul man. Anyone who will use a child for his dark pleasures is evil."

"He was a pedophile, too? Now I am really glad he is no longer on this earth."

"Yes, he is where he belongs," Jason tells her.

"When someone that evil dies, what happens to them? Do they spend eternity in hell as we as Christians are led to believe?"

"When a dark spirit, which is what Milestein

was, dies, they go to the dark side. There is a light side and a dark side. Those who allow their soul to turn dark go to the dark side until they are ready to repent for all the evil they have committed. Only then are they allowed to go home where they will be greeted by our Holy Lord and Savior Jesus Christ, who will bless them thus cleansing the darkness away."

Ronnie sits forward in her chair. "Jason, I am having a hard time seeing you. You are beginning to fade." Her voice fills with fear and sadness.

"Yes, I have allowed my spirit to stay in my empty shell too long. I have to go now, Ronnie," he tells her, the tone of his voice expressing his unwillingness to leave.

"Jason, will you hold me tonight in my dreams?"

"Yes, but only if you *want* me to come to you."

"I wish you could be with me every minute of the night and day, Jason."

"Until I cross over, and make no mistake, the day will come when I have to cross over and go home, I am bound to this house and property."

"I don't want to think about that now. I can't. For now, if you will join me in my dreams and hold me close to you, I will be satisfied."

"Ronnie, there is one more thing I need to make clear. As I already said, I know you want a husband and children. While I can hold you in your dreams, I am unable to satisfy the rest of your needs. You are a healthy young woman with a healthy libido. Being held close in my arms each night will not be enough to satisfy your needs as a woman."

"Why don't we deal with my womanly needs later? However, while we are on the subject of needs, do you still have the needs of a man even though you are not in a human body?"

"Yes, I do. I have made myself deny my needs since there is nothing more I *can* do. I must leave you now, as my substance is all but gone. I will come to you later, my Ronnie."

"Please don't disappoint me." She smiles.

Knowing Ronnie is no longer able to see him, Jason stands across the room watching her as she gets up to put in one of her classic movies. Moving over to the long couch, he sits down to enjoy the movie with her, then grins as he catches the title. It is the 1947 movie classic, *The Ghost and Mrs. Muir.*

CHAPTER NINE

"What is going on with you this morning, Ronnie? You act like this is your first day in front of the camera," Dustin tells her.

"I think I may be coming down with something," she replied.

"Would you rather we wait and do this shoot another time?"

"No, just keep shooting. I'll try to keep it together."

"For someone who doesn't feel up to par, you sure look great."

"Thanks. I'll be all right."

Ronnie jumps as someone slips their arms around her trim waist.

"Didn't mean to frighten you, Ronnie," Nichole tells her, laughing as she spins her around. "Do you see the tall guy with black hair standing over there?" She points to across the way where three very handsome men are enjoying the photoshoot. "He is my date for tonight if you will do me a big favor."

"And that is?"

"Invite me and them to enjoy your pool tonight."

Immediately Jason's face flashes into her mind. "I don't think that is a good idea, Nichole. I have things I need to do this evening, and having guests over would keep me from getting them done."

"Some friend you are, Ronnie. I already told the guys we could come over to your place this evening, and they are looking forward to it."

"Sorry. Sometimes things just don't work out the way you would like them to."

Nichole turns on her heel and, without another word, walks away.

"Guess she doesn't like not getting her way," Dustin says.

"Guess not."

All through the day, Ronnie continues to think about what she now knows about Jason. What bothers her is she cannot confide in anyone about it.

~*~

As soon as she walks through the door, she sees Jason waiting for her.

"I'm glad you're home," he said as he moved towards her.

Ronnie meets him halfway to hold out her arms. "Can I give you a big hug to tell you how glad

I am you're here?"

Without a word, he pulls her into his arms and, to her surprise, covers her mouth with his in a long welcome home kiss.

As they part, she looks up at him, a happy smile covering her face. "That was worth coming home for," she tells him.

"I waited until I saw you drive in before I materialized so we can enjoy our evening together."

"Now, I am looking forward to the rest of our evening. One thing, though, I picked up some fast food for dinner. Do you want to share it with me, or are you still not eating?"

"I will let you enjoy your meal on your own. But *I will* keep you company while you dine." Smiling, he sits down on the stool closest to hers as she places a container of chicken and salad on the island.

Ronnie pours a glass of juice from the fridge then walks back over to take her place on the stool beside his.

"Jason, I want to hear about your life. What you enjoyed growing up. Where you lived. I want to hear all about you."

"You must be bored."

All through the evening, they shared what their life had been like before they met. Even the terrible night Jason's parents were killed in a head-on collision brought on by a drunk driver.

"How terrible that had to be for you. I am surprised that knowing your loved ones await you on the other side that you aren't anxious to go and be with them."

"Yes, it was awful, and yes, I miss them terribly. But I don't want to leave you yet. I am happy to have finally found someone I am content to share my innermost feelings with. But, as I have said, the day will come when I will have to leave you and crossover."

"I don't want to think about that day, Jason. I am already unable to think about being without you."

The sound of the doorbell ringing brings Ronnie to her feet as Jason moves off the stool to walk into the other room.

"I hope this isn't my parents," she scoffs aloud as she makes her way across the floor to open the door.

"Hi Ronnie," Nichole says, throwing her arms wide. "The boys and I decided to come to see you even though you said you didn't want company this evening."

Ronnie can smell liquor on Nichole's breath, and she is sure the men who are with her have been drinking, too.

The dark-haired man Nichole had pointed out to her walked forward. "She insisted we come over. You know Nichole does not take no for an answer," he quietly tells her.

Ronnie's eyes dart across the room to where Jason had been standing to make sure he is no longer there.

"I guess, since you are already here, you can come in." She gives Nichole an annoyed look.

"Oh, come on. Where is your party spirit?" She makes her way over to the bar to begin pouring drinks. "We need to have a few drinks and put on some loud music, and go for a swim." She places the drinks on top of the bar and, reaching down, shoves a CD into the CD player. "No one in the world could throw a pool party like Cory Williams! And now that he is gone, it is left up to you to carry on his legacy!"

To the surprise of all present, Nichole pulls her dress up and over her head to reveal she is wearing nothing underneath. Grabbing her drink from the bar, she runs out the sliding glass door to the pool.

"The last one in the pool is a loser!" she yells, setting her drink down on a glass table before diving headfirst into the pool.

Ronnie can only shake her head as she watches three handsome young men pull off their clothes to join a wild and inebriated Nichole in the pool.

CHAPTER TEN

Ronnie leaves the shower to pull forth a fluffy towel hanging on the towel rack. After slipping a sheer pink nightgown over her head, she reaches out to take a small bottle of her favorite cologne from the shelf to dab a few drops behind each ear and her wrists.

"I want you to enjoy your time by my side, Jason, my dream lover." She laughs aloud.

As she pulls open the bathroom door, she is surprised to see a smiling Jason standing in the hallway.

"Tonight, if you will allow, I would like to hold you in my arms like a real, *alive* man. I won't be able to hold my substance all night, of course, but for as long as I am able, I want to hold you in my arms."

"I would love to be able to feel you lying beside me," Ronnie tells him. "Do you mind if I ask you a question?"

"You may ask me anything you wish. I have nothing, anymore, to hide from you."

"Does your wanting to hold me like a man who is still alive have anything to do with the men who were here and swimming nude in the pool? I am sure you could see what was going on."

"Yes, I could see what was going on. But, more importantly, did *you* find the men attractive and wish *you* could interact with them?

She stopped walking and, turning, looked over at him. "No, I did not want to interact with them. Yes, they are very handsome, all of them, but the man I want to interact with is right here by my side."

"That's all I needed to hear." He grins over at her and, to her surprise, lifts her into his arms to carry her to her room.

Ronnie twines her arms around his neck, lays her head on his shoulder.

When Jason stands her on her feet, she continues to hold onto him, putting her arms around his waist to pull him against her.

"Just think, someday you will be able to tell your grandchildren how you were held in the arms of a ghost one night." His voice fills with bitterness.

Ronnie steps back, staring at him. "What brought on such bitter feelings all of a sudden? I thought we were going to have a night filled with love and tenderness."

"Don't you understand? I want to be with you all the way. I want to make love with you the way a man should with the woman he loves."

Ronnie takes a deep breath to gaze up at him. "Would you like to see if you can make love like a man who is still alive?"

"How do you purpose we do this?" His face fills with love and a little hope. "It is all I can do to keep my substance at top peak. I think that is about all I can hope to achieve. However, I do thank you for wanting to help me."

Ronnie pulls the gown up and over her head, then presses herself against him. "Kiss me, Jason; a manly kiss, not a brotherly kiss. Kiss me like a lover who finds me attractive and desirable."

He tips her face up to cover her mouth with his in a long and passionate kiss that leaves them both wanting when he pulls away.

Ronnie rubs herself against him. "I think you have been deluding yourself in what you can and can't do on this earth."

Without another word, Jason pulls off his clothes and walks her backward to the bed, his hot mouth covering hers all the while.

Ronnie lies down and holds out her arms to him.

Jason moves over her body. "I don't know how long I can keep my body in readiness to make love, but I will do my best to satisfy you."

"That is all I ask."

Ronnie pulls him close to capture one of his nipples in her mouth and smiles as she hears his sharp intake of breath.

"I never knew men could be aroused by having their nipples suckled," he murmured.

Ronnie remains silent as she pleasures his other nipple.

She moves her free hand down to caress his manhood and is surprised when he pulls her hand away.

"Don't you want me to fondle you? I would think it would help you."

"That is just it. I'm afraid it will help me too much. I'm trying to hold onto my feelings as much as possible already, so I won't erupt and leave you wanting."

"Then make love with me, Jason, and allow us both to realize our dreams."

Jason straddles her body, and with a quick snap of his hips, he enters her.

Ronnie surrounds his hips with her long legs to pull him deeper inside her body.

"You are my dream lover, Jason, and the only lover I will ever need the rest of my days on this earth."

"My beautiful Ronnie." He leans forward to kiss her open mouth. "You are my woman. You make me thankful I remained on this plane."

Seeing the passion burning out of control in his eyes, Ronnie pulls his face closer for another long and deep kiss, then moves away as a small scream leaves her throat.

Jason matches her movements then throws back his head as his rigid manhood erupts inside her tightness.

Jason moves his body to lie beside her. "And that, my beautiful Ronnie, is how a ghost makes love with his woman." He smiles over at her.

Ronnie brings one of his hands up to her mouth to place a warm kiss in the middle of his palm.

"You keep that up, and we may have to repeat what we just finished."

"Would that be a hardship for you? It wouldn't be for me." She moves his hand over her passion-filled breast.

"It would not be a hardship at all." He cups her breast in his hand to tweak one hard nipple.

"I have a question for you. Now that we know you can achieve an erection and make mad passionate love with me, do you think there is any chance that you could also make me pregnant?"

"I don't think so since even though I can feel myself ejaculate, there is no ejaculation going into your body. To prove this to yourself, you can touch your womanhood and see that the only moisture comes from your climax."

Ronnie giggles as she snuggles over closer to him. "This is one strange conversation we are having, and now that I am laughing, I think the only thing I can do now is go to sleep."

"I think you're right. Good night, my Ronnie."

"Good night, my dream lover."

CHAPTER ELEVEN

"There she is. The beautiful, talk-of-all-tinsel-town," Dustin says as Ronnie walks into the studio.

"Good morning to you, Dustin. And what pray tell has you so jolly this early in the A.M.?"

"Our esteemed boss just came out of his office looking for you. It seems one of the big news affiliates wants to interview with you concerning as if you can't guess for yourself what went on with you and Waldo Milestein."

"I'll pass. The less I am reminded of that whacko, the better."

"I don't think you can get out of it that easy. When our boss man, who is being invited to be in the interview giving him a chance to have the spotlight shine on the magazine, *he* is the owner of, and *you* are the star model of, I think you are going to be hearing yourself saying, why thank you, I will be glad to interview with you and let you in on all the sorted little details of my hot affair with the stud of Hollywood."

"You are wrong. I have as much clout as the owner of OVER TWENTY MAGAZINE. Remember, I am the niece of the very famous Cory Williams." She smiles, giving him a view of her beautiful white and even teeth.

"I guess we're about to find out since here he comes, and we know *he ain't lookin' for me.*"

"Ronnie, just the beauty I am looking for." Mr. Rainier gives her a big hug.

"And why are you looking for me, Mr. Rainier?"

"I think we'll be more comfortable in my office with a nice cup of coffee to relax you."

Dustin flips his fingers in the direction of the office, earning him a sour look from Ronnie.

Ronnie pulls a chair up to the desk to take the cup of coffee Rainier hands to her.

"I have some very exciting news for you, Ronnie. You and I are going to be on TV in an interview. A big news affiliate wants to interview about your relationship with Waldo Milestein."

"There was no relationship between myself and Milestein."

Rainier cocks his head, a smug look covering his face. "Oh, come now, Ronnie. If Milestein and you had not had a relationship, he would not have taken it upon himself to make the long trip to your home that sits in the middle of nowhere."

"You and everyone else can believe what you want to believe. I said there was no relationship between Waldo the Walrus and myself. Now," a slight chill resonates in her otherwise, quiet voice, "if there isn't anything more you need to talk with me about, I will be getting back to the job you are paying me to do."

"Are you saying you are refusing to do this interview? This interview could put OVER TWENTY MAGAZINE at the top in sales, not to mention all the free advertising!"

Ronnie stands and sets her coffee on the desk. "Since there *is* no story, there is no reason for me to waste my time doing an interview that is only going to drag my name and the name of my family through the mud."

"I thought this job was important to you, Ronnie." An angry tone creeps into Rainier's voice. "I can see how I was wrong."

"This job is important to me, Mr. Rainier. As the niece of the famous actor Cory Williams, the heartthrob of millions of women the world over, I guess being in front of the camera runs in the blood."

"Yes, I see your point," Rainier said. The anger is gone now from his voice as he walks behind his desk.

"Is our conversation over?"

"Yes, you can get back to work while I call and cancel the interview." His voice echoes his disappointment.

As Ronnie walks out of the office, Nichole comes running over to her.

"Dustin just filled me in on the latest scoop. You are going to be interviewing along with the boss on one of the big news outlets? Oh my god! I would give my virginity to get a request like that!"

"I think that was traded years ago, Nichole, but we won't...*get into it*. Pardon the pun." Dustin laughs aloud.

"Shut the fuck up, Dustin. You're just jealous you weren't the first. I want to hear what Ronnie has to say about the interview."

"There is not going to be an interview. Since there is no story, there is no reason for an interview," Ronnie tells them.

"You can't be saying that you turned down an interview to be on TV!" Nichole's dark eyes are alive with shock and disbelief.

"Why can't she turn down an interview on TV? She turned down a role in a movie!" Dustin's voice is quiet and to the point.

"Why do you get all the breaks, Ronnie? I am right up there with you in the looks department. I make as much money as you. I get just as many requests for a photo layout as you. And yet, you get all the breaks. I just wish I could get my face seen by millions. You can bet your sweet ass I would not turn them down."

"Trust me, I didn't ask for that interview. I would not trust that station to do a real sit-down anyway. By the time they were through editing the whole thing, they would make it look like I had affairs with most of the fat slugs in Hollywood."

"Maybe *you* haven't been cuddling up to the right slugs, Nichole," Dustin tells her, a cheesy smile splitting the corners of his full mouth as he continues setting up his equipment.

"We're talking about me, Dustin, not you. You would hump any peter-nipper who looked your way if it would get you...*ahead* in your field."

"Since we all three need to get to work," his cold gaze moves over Nicole, "I'll ignore that remark to make a suggestion."

Ronnie and Nichole turn to look over at him.

"If you both want to get noticed by the big wigs out in fairy tale land, which anyone with eyes to see knows you do, why don't you allow the boss to set up an interview with a news affiliate that wouldn't taint the interview? Hell, Ronnie, you own the house that belonged to one of the biggest stars in Hollywood. Let the fans see the house and grounds. Invite some big stars to spend a weekend and throw a big pool party just like Cory used to do."

"I don't think so, Dustin." Ronnie laughs aloud. "I doubt the boss would want to be naked in a pool with a bunch of gay men flashing the cameras and, too, I would not be comfortable with a bunch of spoiled Hollywood bigheads all wanting to be waited on at the same time."

"Oh, come on, Ronnie. I think it's a great idea. And too, you could talk about the house being haunted by the handsome male ghost that Cory always told us about."

"Cory made that story up. He told the story to get the film producers to use his house in a film."

"Are you sure, Ronnie? I heard Cory tell that story many times, and it sure didn't sound as though he was making it up," Nichole said.

"Believe me, Nichole, since I am the one who lives in the house, if there was a ghost there, I would know it."

"Wouldn't it be cool if there was a ghost there and he was good-looking and sexy? You could have a real dream lover." Nichole laughs as she sees the shocked look on Ronnie's face.

"If there was a ghost living in Ronnie's house, he wouldn't be coming onto our Ronnie, although he would have to be deaf and blind not to. He might come onto Ronnie's new boyfriend." Dustin grins over at her.

"So you are seeing someone. I can't wait to meet

him," Nichole tells her.

"I doubt you would be impressed. He isn't your type of guy."

"But anyway, getting back to you doing an interview in your house, I think it is a great idea, and if I was you, I would tell the boss about the idea so he could be included," Dustin says, setting up the camera for the day's photo shoot.

"Tell me about what?" Mr. Rainier asks, walking into the studio.

"Ronnie told us she is not going to do the TV interview, and I said that since she is not doing *that* interview, she could interview with a real journalist at Cory William's former house. Given that Ronnie now owns the house, it would be an even bigger interview than the one she turned down. And of course, you and the magazine would be included in the interview," Dustin says.

"Good god! That *is* a sensational idea. I am impressed, Dustin. Sometimes you surprise me."

"Thank you, Mr. Rainier. I always like to help out when I can."

"When would you like to get this interview underway, Ronnie?"

"I will have to give this some thought, Mr. Rainier. I like to keep my personal life private, and that goes for my home, too."

"You aren't telling me you intend to turn down

this interview too? You know as well as I do that any news affiliate will jump on the chance to film an interview in the former house of such a big star as Cory Williams. You are his niece. Cash in on such sensationalism. It can only help your career." Rainier stands looking at her.

"As I said, I will have to give this some thought. Right now, I would like to get to work."

CHAPTER TWELVE

Seated together on one of the couches in the beautifully decorated living room, Ronnie turns to look at Jason.

"My boss at the studio wanted to set up an interview with one of the big news affiliates on TV to discuss my relationship with Milestein. Of course, it would be a big coup for Mr. Rainier and the magazine. I turned down the interview."

"Do you think that was wise, Ronnie, given this could help your career?"

"The news affiliate wanting to do the interview is one that never vets their stories. Since there was no relationship with Milestein, I saw no need for an interview."

"In that case, I feel you were within your rights to turn the interview down."

"My cameraman, Dustin, had come up with an idea that would still put the boss in the limelight and still get a story on the air for the magazine."

"What is his idea?"

"He thinks it would be good to have an interview here. Not about Milestein, although, since this is where he breathed his last, it would come up. He thinks the story could center on the ghost Cory would tell about to entertain his guests in the late hours of the night after the pool party wound down."

"What do you think about this idea?"

"Again, since this is another untruth that my uncle used to get a film producer to use this house in one of his movies, I think it is a waste of time and money. There is no gay ghost roaming around who liked to harass the male guests." Ronnie laughs aloud.

"Are you sure about that, Ronnie?"

Ronnie turns, staring at Jason. "Are you telling me the story is true?"

"Yes, I am telling you that the story is true. His name is Leonard Wellesley. He died right here on the estate during a late-night pool party where he slipped and fell on the slippery slate of the pool deck. He was very drunk. There were very few guests still here, and the ones who were, had gone inside, so no one knew he needed help. Paramedics, who treated him, theorized that since there was blood on the slate, that he most likely slipped, hitting his head then fell over unconscious, into the pool."

Ronnie gets to her feet to walk over to the bar.

"I need a drink. Do you want to join me? Up to you."

"Yeah, as a matter of fact, I will have a drink with you. I'll have a shot of scotch. No ice. I'm finding it interesting to know what all I am still able to do."

"Then all those stories Uncle Cory told about a gay ghost were true? Did he see and talk with this person after he died? And, too, were you there the night the accident happened?"

"As a matter-of-fact, I was here that night."

"Then I sure hope my new-found house guest doesn't try and bother me. I am not into ghosts and things I can't see. No offense, Jason. I can see you."

"I can assure you that Leonard will behave himself. He was very close to Cory." Jason grins when he catches the look Ronnie aims at him. "I mean that in a platonic way only, Ronnie."

"I am glad you clarified that bit of news. I don't want any visuals."

"Are you going to allow the interview here?"

"I guess I could. But what about you? What if the camera picks up your image? It has been known to happen," Ronnie tells him, a serious look on her face.

"I will be sure and stay clear of the mansion that night and too, I will be sure and keep Leonard away."

As her phone begins to ring, Ronnie picks it up, punches the talk button, and puts the call on speakerphone.

"Hello."

"Hi, Ronnie. This is Mom. I just talked with Mr. Rainier, and he told me about the interview that you turned down with one of the big news affiliates. Why are you trying to sabotage your career? I would think after that mess with Milestein that you would be happy to have your beautiful face seen by millions of viewers on TV," Raquel tells her.

"I realize you are upset, Mom, but I was not about to have one of the biggest fake news affiliates interview with me. They would have *ruined* my career with all their lies not made it more popular."

"Mr. Rainier said you are thinking about doing an interview at the mansion. I certainly hope you are going to do more than just *think* about this interview."

"I will let you know what I decide. If I do decide to allow an interview here, I will be sure and have you and dad here so you can both get your faces on TV."

Ronnie holds her cell phone against her chest for a moment so her mother can't hear her laughing.

"That is very giving of you, Ronnie," Raquel says. All anger was now gone from her voice. "However, as much as I appreciate the offer to have us join you, I doubt very seriously if your dad will accept. I, of course, will be glad to accept your kind offer."

"You never know, we might get lucky, and the ghost that Uncle Cory always told stories about might show up. Could be a good thing and scare all those here so much that the interview would be talked about on all the stations and make the fake news stations jealous they didn't get to be here for the interview."

"Ronnie, please, there is no such thing as a ghost."

"I don't agree. Speaking for myself, I believe anything is possible. There is too much out there that we don't know about. What would be funny is if Uncle Cory and the gay ghost both show up and scare the bejesus out of all the film crew."

"Okay, since I have to be going, I'll leave you with that thought. Keep me posted on what you decide to do," Raquel says.

"I will. Love and hugs to you and Dad."

Ronnie turns off the phone, slips the phone into her pocket.

"Sounds as though you are leaning on going ahead with the interview here at the mansion," Jason speaks up, accepting the shot glass of Scotch Ronnie hands to him.

Ronnie turns to sit back down on the couch when she catches sight of someone standing in the hallway.

"What's wrong?" Jason leans forward on the couch.

"Someone is standing in the hallway," she whispers.

Jason gets to his feet to look to where she is pointing. "All right, Leonard, you can stop hiding. We know you are here. You need to come over here and let Ronnie see you."

A man in his late twenties of medium height and weight comes forward. "I'm sorry if I frightened you, Miss Westerlyne. I would never do anything to hurt someone related to my best friend, Cory Williams."

"I'll forgive you this time, but I don't want you roaming around the house. This is my house now, and I say what is and isn't allowed here, Leonard," Ronnie tells him. "And you can call me Ronnie."

"Thank you, Ronnie."

Leonard walks across the room to flop down in an overstuffed chair. "I'm glad you aren't telling me that I can't come here anymore. That would make me very sad. Cory and I could sit and talk the night away. I miss him so much. I tried to talk him out of going home to the other side, but he said he needed to be with those who have gone on before."

"Don't you think that is where you belong, too? I hear it is very beautiful there," Ronnie says.

"Yeah, I know. Cory has come back to visit, and he tries to talk me into going back with him. I'm just not ready to go yet, even though I hate being a ghost."

"What is it about being a ghost that you hate, Leonard?"

"I can't do any of the fun things I used to do

like enjoying dining in the best restaurants, availing myself of the finest foods, drinking the night away with friends, or being with a handsome young man. My only pleasure now is scaring the hell of people who can't see me unless I want them to."

We're enjoying a drink. Would you care to join us?"

"Ronnie, I am a ghost. A ghost cannot drink or eat."

"Leonard," Jason says, holding up a shot-glass partially filled with Scotch, "I'm a ghost, and I am enjoying a drink."

Leonard gets to his feet, a smile lighting up his handsome face, to walk over to the bar. "Maybe being a ghost doesn't have to be such a bad thing after all."

"Our staying on this plane for any length of time is not good for our wellbeing," Jason says. "What is keeping you here, Leonard?"

Leonard tips his glass to his mouth. "I guess I just got used to being here. I always enjoyed my talks with Cory while he was here. We had a lot of laughs, and I miss him like hell."

"My Uncle Cory was a good man. While at first, I had a hard time accepting his lifestyle, in the years passed, I'm able to reconcile with his choice in how he lived his life."

"Yes, sometimes life takes a turn, and we either accept that person for who they are or lose out on knowing them. I lucked out in my parents' being acceptable of my being gay. I kept my private life separate from theirs, and it worked out," Leonard tells them, throwing a half-filled glass of scotch down his throat.

"Leonard, I would go easy on the liquor if I were you. You are not used to drinking, so you might find that you react differently to alcohol now," Jason warns him.

Leonard turns to come back to his chair. "I'm fine. I have always been able to handle my liquor, and since what I drink can have no big effect on me, I will thank you to keep your concerns for my wellbeing to yourself."

"What did you do?" Jason stands up. "We can't see you anymore. We can hear you, but you have completely disappeared."

"I guess this could be why ghosts can't drink. Although you are drinking, Jason, and I can still see you." Leonard laughs. His disembodied voice sounding eerie in the room.

"I am still sipping on my first drink. I don't try and drink up the entire bar. This could be the reason I can still hold my essence."

"Okay, I guess we can go with that."

Ronnie draws back in shock as she sees one of the bottles sitting on the bar lift and the stopper pop up, then slowly land on the bar. The bottle tips over a glass. When the glass is almost full, the bottle gently sits back down on the bar, and the stopper slowly falls back into the bottle.

"I guess, since I intend to enjoy this night being a bit more than tipsy followed with an enjoyable dip in the pool which cannot do me more harm, you can rest assured you won't be seeing my handsome self anymore this night."

"That's nice to know," Jason whispers.

"I promise not to be a voyeur *tonight*," he tells them with a devilish laugh.

"You don't think Leonard has been spying on us in the bedroom, do you?" Ronnie whispers, uneasiness sounding in her voice.

"If he has been, he won't anymore. I will forbid him to be able to come into our room or the bathroom."

"How can you stop him?"

"*I* probably can't, but I know someone who can. There are rules in the spirit world, and when someone breaks one of the rules, he or she has to be held accountable."

"Are you talking about my Uncle Cory?"

"Yes. I think now that Cory has been on the other side for a while, and given the love and respect that Leonard has for Cory, I think that he can talk Leonard over to the light."

They both jump as male laughter is heard in the surrounding silence. "I wouldn't bet on that if I was you," Leonard murmurs to himself.

CHAPTER THIRTEEN

Ronnie gets out of her car and clicks the alarm.

"Wait up there, beautiful lady, and I'll walk into the studio with you," Dustin calls out to her.

"Good morning, Dustin."

"Good morning to you, Sunshine." He draws back, looking at her. "I don't see that happy smile I have been seeing here of late. Did something happen in snuggleberg I need to know about?"

Ronnie smiles at him. "No, just a little tired this morning. I didn't sleep well last night."

"You know I am always there for you anytime you need to be rocked," he tells her, his voice low and sensual. He drapes an arm around her shoulders. "So tell me, when do we get to meet this man who has stolen the heart of a woman I have lusted for since I laid eyes on her? Or, could I be lucky enough to find he is no longer a threat?"

"To answer your questions, my new friend is

still very much in the picture, but when you can meet him, it is going to be a while. He is a very private person," she laughs quietly at the curious look on his face.

"Ronnie, I don't want to try and tell you how to run your life, but it has been my experience that when someone tries to alienate you from your friends, that is someone you need to distance yourself from."

"Thank you, Dustin, for your excellent advice, but this man is not someone who wants to keep me away from my love ones."

As the two walk into the studio, Mr. Rainier steps out of his office. "Dustin, you can go ahead and get things lined up for today's shoot," he tells the man, waiting to hear what is needed before turning his attention to Ronnie. "Ronnie, I need to talk with you in my office."

Ronnie sits down in a chair facing Rainier's desk and crosses her long legs.

"I am interested in hearing your view on Dustin's idea about having the interview at your house since you turned down our being on the news with a journalist."

"I am giving the idea some serious thought as long as the one doing the interview is Sean Flannery from Wolf News. I want the interview handled with class. My Uncle Cory Williams was a big star. I want his fans to be happy with the interview."

"I agree with you. Now on to the big question. Am I going to be there for the interview?"

"If I do the interview, you will be there with me," she tells him, laughing slightly as a happy, boy-like smile spreads across his face.

"Then, as soon as you make up your mind, you can let me know. This will go a long way in advertising the magazine. I appreciate your giving attitude, Ronnie."

"I will keep you apprised of my decision, Mr. Rainier."

Ronnie pushes back her chair to get to her feet, smiling as Rainier rushes from behind his desk to open the office door for her.

As Ronnie walks out of the office, Nichole hurries forward to pull her off to the side. "So, did you agree to do the interview in your home, as Mr. Rainier wants you to do?"

"How do you know what Rainier and I talked about?" Ronnie drew back, grinning at her.

"Oh well..sometimes he and I talk away from the studio," Nichole stammers.

"Sounds to me like old man Rainier is dippin' into the honey hive," Dustin snickers, looking around.

"Dustin, if you want to keep your job, you will watch your mouth and know when to mind your own business." Nichole's voice sizzles.

"All right, you two, we have work to do, so let's

get to it." Ronnie makes her way to the dressing room.

"Just one more thing, though, Nicole, if you ever find yourself in need of a backup when the old boy's steed ain't up to givin' bareback rides, I am only a phone call away. My stallion never lets *me* down." He gives his crotch a gentle pat as he leers down at her.

"You're disgusting," she tells him, a little smile tugging at her full mouth.

"You're as good as in the sack, baby," Dustin murmurs. He walks over to the camera as he sees Ronnie walk out of the dressing room dressed in a short, blue-green dress that shows off her tight body while at the same time keeps her look of class.

Dustin nods as each click of the camera catches the serene glow covering the beautiful face of the young woman giving the appearance of walking up a busy street.

"Keep that look, Ronnie," Dustin calls out to her.

"She is one beautiful woman," Rainier stands quietly watching. "Makes you wonder who she is thinking of to give off such complete luminosity."

"She told me she is seeing a new man. I guess she is completely enthralled with him."

"Maybe, if we can pull off this interview at the mansion, we'll get to meet him."

"Maybe, but I wouldn't bank on it. Seems he is

not into meeting new people. A funny thing, though. When she told me his name and that he had been a stuntman in a few of Cory Williams' films, I thought she was putting me on."

"Why's that?"

"She said his name is Jason. The only Jason I know who was a stuntman in Williams' films was Jason Talbert."

"So? What's so strange about that?" Rainier asked, beginning to move away.

"Jason Talbert was killed sometime back in a fatal accident while performing a very dangerous stunt in Williams' last film. It was in all the papers and over the news."

"Guess she has to be talking about another Jason. She sure as hell can't be dating a ghost."

Dustin laughs outright. "No ghost could put a smile on Ronnie's face like she wears almost every morning she walks in here. That would take a real stud."

Rainier looks at him then walks away back to his office.

"Okay, my beauty," Dustin turns off the camera. "I think we have all we need for today. As always, you gave a bang-up performance. Even the boss watched the shoot."

"Thanks, Dustin. I'll go change, then go home."

"Hold up a moment, Ronnie."

Ronnie turns back, waiting to see what else Dustin needed.

"I didn't think you'd mind my telling Rainier about you seeing someone. Like me, he was wondering who it is that can put such a glow on your beautiful face. You said his name was Jason and that he was once a stuntman in some of your uncle's films. I told him the only Jason I knew of was Jason Talbert, who died in a bad accident while working in Cory's last film."

"No, you misunderstood me when I said his name," she thinks fast, "It is Jansen. Also, he *wanted* to be a stuntman but found he didn't have the nerve it takes to be one. I was mistaken too, as I thought he said he had already been a stuntman in one of Uncle Cory's films." She forced a slight laugh.

"Hmmm, I could have sworn you said Jason. But I guess I could have heard wrong since the two names are so similar."

"No problem." She turns away.

"I told the boss there is no way in hell you could have meant Jason Talbert. No ghost could put a smile on a woman's face like the one you come into work wearing."

Ronnie waves him away, laughing on her way to the dressing room.

CHAPTER FOURTEEN

Jason sits down on the side of the pool, sticks his feet into the water, content to sit quietly for a while until Ronnie returns home.

"I don't want to intrude if you would rather be alone," Leonard tells him as he stands looking down at Jason.

"No, it's all right. You're the one in my thoughts at the moment."

Leonard laughs outright. "I didn't know you cared, Jason. I thought you only filled your thoughts with the lovely Ronnie."

"My thoughts centered on how long you intend to stick around here instead of going back home. You know you have a lot of loved ones awaiting your return."

"The same can be said for you, Jason. Although your reasons for remaining on this side are quite clear. But why did you choose to remain before Ronnie came into the picture?"

Jason looks up at him for a moment, then turns away. "Cory asked if I would stick around for a while to keep an eye on Ronnie."

"Because he knew I was still hanging around?" A slight bitterness crept into Leonard's tone.

"He didn't say why, but you could be the reason. Cory knows what a prankster you are, and he did not want you scaring Ronnie."

"Very astute man was our Cory."

"Now you can tell me the reason you aren't going back home to the other side."

"I don't have a reason. Right now, I am enjoying being here."

Jason gets to his feet. "You know being gay is no reason for you to fear going home. Weren't you gay during your other lifetimes?"

"No. This is the first lifetime I have ever wanted to be with my sex."

"What is different about this lifetime? Didn't you choose a gay life before coming back? I know you have to be aware that every spirit who wants to return to this side has to plot out their entire life before The Holy Council of Elders will give their okay for the return.

"Are you trying to make me believe you put meeting Ronnie and staying here after your spirit left your body into *your* life plot?"

"I'm going to go inside and have a drink. Care to join me?"

Nodding, Leonard follows behind as Jason walks into the house and up to the bar.

"One thing we can all say about Cory is he only stocked the best liquor." Leonard grins.

"Yeah, I keep hearing this."

After filling their glasses with their favorite drinks, they head back outside to the pool.

"I don't know about you, but I notice I am finding it easier and easier to hold my form. I prefer being able to see myself and you."

"I agree. Now, I'll answer your question about Ronnie. No, I did not add my staying on this side longer than I should have. Then I am sure The Holy Council will take into consideration that sometimes in this life, things don't always work out as planned. Now, let's get back to what we were discussing. You were saying this is the first time you wanted to be with a man. Can you tell me why? I am not going to judge you, Leonard."

Leonard takes a deep swallow of his drink then looks over at Jason. "Of all my lifetimes, and I have had many, this is the first lifetime I was ever really in love."

"How could you go through different lifetimes and not know the reason you were never able to fall in love is that you are gay?"

"I guess I just kept blaming my inability to enjoy having sex with a female on having a low libido."

"Why didn't you come back into this lifetime as a female? Since you want to have a relationship with males instead of females, don't you think that would have solved your problem?"

"I hope you're not going to fall back on the joke about men saying they plan to come back next time as a hooker so they can get all the sex they want."

Jason gives him a long look, then turns away.

"Anyway, growing up, I always played with trucks, guns, and male toys. We keep hearing that gay men grew up wanting to play with dolls and girl toys. I believe that is a fallacy."

"All right, how did you come to fall in love with a male letting you know you are and always have been gay?"

"The moment I first laid eyes on Cory Williams. It was as though I had known him all my life. We became close friends and then lovers."

"I didn't know that Cory was gay," Jason says, giving Leonard his undivided attention.

"You worked with the man and never knew he was gay? Guess you aren't very astute, Jason, my friend." Leonard laughs outright. "But to be completely honest, Cory was bisexual. While I had a difficult time reconciling his wanting to be with others, I consoled my wounded heart with the fact that at least he did not want to be with other men. If that makes sense." He turns away, but not before Jason could see the tears he was trying to wipe away.

"How do you feel about parents wanting to change the sex of their children just because they want to dress up in clothes opposite to their gender and play with toys always thought to be of interest to the opposite sex?"

"I would say, parents who want to change a child's sex, especially when that child is very young, is a parent who has a problem identifying with aging and being a grandparent. They are only thinking of themselves, not the child."

"I am finding all this very interesting, but here is something I do not understand. If you were so in love with Cory, why are you still staying here instead of returning to the other side where Cory is?"

"If you want the truth, I guess I am afraid of being refused entrance on the other side since I didn't follow the rules and map out the life I would lead in this lifetime."

"Leonard, if you want my advice on what you can do, I would call on Cory to come and visit you and tell him what your fears are about returning home to the other side. I bet he will be able to put your fears to rest."

"All right, I'll try it your way. Cory always comes when I call him."

They both look up as Ronnie walks out to the pool in a blue bikini that shows off her well-endowed figure.

"If ever a man needed an assessment to see if he is gay, Ronnie would be a good tester. If that much beauty doesn't jerk up the Johnson," Jason delivers with a wide grin on his face, "nothing will."

"I see you two are enjoying yourselves," Ronnie told them before climbing up the ladder to the diving board to dive headfirst into the pool.

They both move over to the side of the pool as Ronnie's head bobs to the top of the water.

"Yes, enjoying your liquor. I hope you don't mind our helping ourselves," Jason says, smiling down at her.

"No, I don't care if you enjoy yourselves while I am away from the house. There is enough liquor to keep you happy, so enjoy."

"I hope your day was busy and fruitful," Leonard tells her.

"Yes, I had a good day." Ronnie swims over to the rounded steps leading from the pool to seat herself in one of the lawn chairs.

"Ronnie, why don't I go and pour you a cold drink from the bar and bring it out to you." Leonard comes forward.

"I would like that, Leonard, and thank you for offering. I will have a double scotch and water with very little ice."

"Coming right up." He turns toward the sliding glass door leading into the house.

"I'm happy you're home, my love," Jason whispers as he bends down to place a soft kiss on her parted lips.

Ronnie returns his kiss, a pleased smile covering her face. "I need to talk with both of you while I have the chance."

Leonard sets her drink down on the glass table beside her chair.

"I have decided to allow a news affiliate to give me an interview here at the mansion. I don't know if you both want to be present while the cameras are rolling. The camera could pick up your energy. It has been known to happen, so I will leave it up to you to decide."

"You might like to know that your Uncle Corey is going to be here sometime. Leonard wants to talk with him. I know you won't mind him paying a visit here."

"Of course not," Ronnie says, "what's one more ghost added to our happy group?"

"Not to be overbearing, but since Corey has already transcended to the other side, he is considered a spirit, not a ghost. Only Jason and I are ghosts."

"I guess I need to brush up on my other-worldly etiquette," Ronnie says, not bothering to wipe the wide grin from her face. "In all seriousness, though, I would prefer that the two of you leave the liquor alone until after the interview is over, and the news crew has all left."

"You have our word we will be on our best behavior. No use tempting things to go wrong," Leonard says.

"I will hold you to your word, Leonard. With two ghosts and a spirit in the house, we need all the good luck we can call on to get through this interview that will be shown all over the country."

CHAPTER FIFTEEN

This is so exciting; I can't tell you how much I appreciate you allowing me to be here." Raquel giggles. Her giddiness making her sound more like a teenager instead of the mother of a grown woman.

"I told you that both you and Dad are welcome to be here. I wish *I* didn't have to be here." She bent forward, brushing her long hair underneath, then straightened up, throwing her head back to allow the silken strands to fall down her slender back. "By allowing a real news affiliate to do the interview, I am hoping there will be fewer questions about Milestein."

"I wouldn't get my hopes up about that. That slob is still big news now that it is coming out what a user of young men and women he was."

A young girl tapped on the downstairs bathroom door.

Raquel pulled open the door to see what she needed.

"Sorry to bother you, but we are about ready to do the interview," she said quietly.

"Thanks. She'll be right out."

"Guess we can't put it off any longer," Ronnie says, allowing her mother to go ahead of her out of the room.

The girl who had tapped on the door directed Ronnie to be seated in a chair in the living room, then quickly moved another chair at an angle to seat a man Ronnie recognized.

"It's an honor to meet you, Miss Westerlyne. I was a big fan of your Uncle Cory Williams. And while we're on the subject of your famous uncle, I have always wanted to check out this house." He chuckled, looking around.

"I have always been a big fan of yours, Mr. Flannery, and please call me Ronnie," she told him."

"Only if you'll call me Sean." He clasped the hand she holds out to him.

Ronnie looks at him and then looks away.

"Is something wrong, Ronnie? I detect a slight unease. You have no reason to be nervous. A woman with your experience of being before the camera should be used to this by now."

"I know the subject of Milestein will have to come up since this is where he breathed his last, but I would appreciate it if you don't belabor the fact."

"You have my word on it, Ronnie. I will be as

brief as I can."

"I appreciate it, Sean. I knew I could count on you to have my back," Ronnie says.

"We aim to please at Wolf News." He gives her a pleased grin.

One of the cameramen walks over to where Ronnie is seated. "Miss Westerlyne, I don't mean to interrupt your conversation, but could you please ask the man walking around the room to please be seated. I am trying to get the right camera angle on you and Sean, and his stepping in front of the camera is not helping me," he says, not bothering to hide the annoyance in his tone of voice.

Ronnie can feel her stomach tighten. "What does the man look like so I will know who you are referring to?"

"There he is." The cameraman motions the man in question forward. "You need to go have a seat and stay out of the way of the camera," he tells him.

"Sorry," a man of average height and very handsome responds, moving across the room to stand in front of Ronnie. "I am trying to get the food you ordered, Miss Westerlyne, set up on the dining room table and the extra glasses lined up on the island." His voice is apologetic.

"Thank you for all your help," Ronnie tells him, holding out her hand to him, a pleased and relaxed smile spreading across her face.

"Also, I brought along some wooden tables to place beside the outside lawn chairs set up around the pool. Glass tables are too much of a hazard, especially when alcohol is served. I'll go ahead and put the glass tables in the garage until the interview is over, then set the glass tables back up for you."

"I'll tell you what. What is your name?" Ronnie asks him.

"My name is Brad," he tells her, a wide grin spreading across his handsome face.

"I am glad to meet you, Brad. What would you say to our swapping my glass tables for your wooden tables?"

"I would have no problem with it, but my tables are just cheap little wooden ones I picked up at a yard sale. I can tell by the looks of your glass tables you paid a pretty penny for them." He starts to walk away then turns back. "I can't tell you how much I have wanted to check out this house. All the stories floating around about the parties and the gay ghost who liked to scare the guests. I sure would have liked to have met him. I so wish my partner could have come with me this evening. When I tell him all about how beautiful the house is and that I got to meet you and Mr. Flannery, who is my favorite star on Wolf News, he is just going to be green with envy."

"Why don't you give your friend a call and tell him I said he is welcome to join us."

"Oh my god!" His voice is filled with exciting laugher. "Are you serious?"

"Yes, go give him a call and tell him to hurry on over so he doesn't miss anything," Ronnie says, her voice filled with amusement.

As Brad moves quickly towards the front door, Sean leans forward, speaking in a low tone of voice. "That was very nice of you to do that for Brad. I have to tell you when I found out the crew and I was going to do an interview in the old Cory Williams house, I was beside myself with excitement, too. That story about the gay ghost has been around for quite some time."

"Yes, my Uncle Cory was quite the storyteller."

"Miss Westerlyne, Sean, we're ready to shoot the interview, so you need to sit back and get comfortable," the camera operator informs them. "Four three two one!" He points a finger in their direction.

"Good evening. Tonight we are interviewing a very special guest. Ronnie Westerlyne is the niece of the very famous actor and heartthrob of millions of panting females, Cory Williams. As you can see by looking at this vision of loveliness and to quote an old saying," Sean reaches a hand out to Ronnie, "the apple did not fall far from the tree in the looks department."

"Thank you, Sean, and let me say," she smiles as her sexy voice flows over him, "I could not ask for a more handsome man to be doing an interview with."

The camera angles in close to capture the bright flush moving up Sean's face.

"Now I'm going to be sitting here with a red face and a stammer stutter in my voice trying to conduct an interview with one of the top models of The Over Twenty Magazine." He laughs openly.

"Thank you, Sean, and speaking of The Over Twenty Magazine, we have with us this evening, Mr. Rainier, the owner of the popular magazine."

Ronnie looks across the room and holds out her hand. "Mr. Rainier, why don't you join us? I am sure the millions of fans of The Over Twenty Magazine would love to get a look at the man who gives the fashionably conscious, so many great ideas on how to dress for any occasion."

Mr. Rainier walks over to take the hand of both Ronnie and Sean, his face showing how pleased he is to be in the spotlight.

"Thank you both for inviting me to be a part of this very important and long-awaited interview."

Sean directs Rainier to one of the chairs nearby.

"I am very pleased to be talking with the man my daughter has so much respect for. You are a very important man in the Flannery House," Sean tells him.

"Sounds like your daughter is a fan of The Over Twenty Magazine. I am happy to say that the magazine has helped many young girls in knowing how to dress to attain that sought-after job in today's work environment.

"She is, and I must say she makes her mother and me very proud with her style of dress. No torn jeans for her. She is a young lady with class, and her choice of chic clothing shows it."

"I am so glad to be a part of the well-dressed young woman of today."

"Your reputation is well-founded, Mr. Rainier." Sean holds out his hand.

As the camera zeroes in on a close-up of the interview host, Rainier discreetly leaves his chair to walk back across the room.

"Ronnie, I am sure you are aware of how much our viewers want to hear about what happened in this house that some believe is the catalyst in Waldo Milestein's death. It has been rumored that Milestein came here to offer you a part in his upcoming film, and you turned him down, an offer that a lot of young women would sell their souls to have."

"Milestein came to my house, but he did not come with simply an offer for a role in his upcoming film. That is what the other news networks wrongly use to boost their ratings, and this is why when I was approached to do an interview with such a news station, I refused. When offered a chance to do an interview with a reputable news affiliate, an affiliate who vets their stories before airing them, I accepted. I accepted so I can put to rest the rumors that I was having an affair with Waldo Milestein."

"What was the other reason Milestein came to your house, Ronnie?"

Ronnie looks straight into the camera. "He came thinking that I would have sex with him. When I refused, he threatened to ruin my career as a top model with The Over Twenty Magazine."

The camera pans in on the disgusted look covering Sean's face. "What happened when you refused his offer of a movie role and his request to have sex with you?"

"He became very angry. In fact, he became so angry that he threatened my life."

"Waldo Milestein actually threatened your life!" Sean leans forward in his chair.

"Yes. He said that since my home is far out and in the middle of 100-acres, no one would ever find my body."

"You must have been scared to death, knowing you are all alone at the hands of a man threatening your life."

"Oddly enough, I was more angry than I was afraid. As we all know, Waldo Milestein was a very obese man. The thought of him putting his fat hands on me made me literally sick to my stomach."

"How did you get away from him?" Sean asked,

looking around the quiet room as the camera spans the horrified faces of those watching the interview.

"We heard the doorbell ring, and as I started to run, Milestein grabbed me, putting his hand over my mouth. He warned me to be quiet so whoever it was would think I was not in the house, even though my car and his car were in the driveway."

"Oh my god. This is like something straight out of a horror movie."

"It was. While he held me imprisoned against him, I could feel his hot breath on the side of my neck. Knowing I had to do something in order to save my life, I reached my hand back to grab his testicles and squeeze. As any man knows, this works. I learned this in some of the programs offered to women on how to protect themselves. I would tell all women to get into some of these programs, especially if you live alone."

"Ouch!" Sean snickers, but I heartily agree. A woman alone can never be too careful. Now, just so we don't keep our listening audience sitting on the edge of their chairs, who was at the door?"

"A good friend of mine was there to join me in watching some of my classic movies. I have to laugh when I think about what Milestein must have thought upon seeing my savior. My friend's name is Jansen, and he looks so much like Jason Talbert, a stuntman who worked in some of my Uncle Cory's films that they could be twins. This is probably what brought on

Milestein's heart attack as Jason Talbert died sometime back in a terrible accident while on the movie set. His funeral was packed with everyone who was anyone, including Milestein. Milestein must have thought he was seeing a ghost."

Sean joins Ronnie and the rest of those in the room in amused laughter.

"I don't doubt you are right in what Milestein thought was happening. And, now that you have mentioned a ghost in the house, what can you tell me about all the stories Cory Williams would regale his late-night guests with?"

"Ah yes," she smiles," my Uncle Cory was not only a great actor, but he was also a masterful storyteller. At the time the stories came about, he was trying to get the film producer to use this house in one of his films. Which by the way, he was able to bring about, by telling the producer that there was a gay ghost who loved to pester the men and the women who would come to the parties in the house."

"So you are saying that the gay ghost story was just that, a made-up story?"

"Sean, are you going to sit here and tell everyone in TV America that you believe in ghosts?"

For the first time in his career as a news commentator, Sean Flannery was speechless.

~*~

Later that evening, Ronnie and Raquel were

standing at the bar, enjoying the quiet.

"Ronnie, I think the interview went very well. I believe you explained what happened here with Milestein in an unrestrained way. Of course, those in the Hollywood scene will try and make people believe that Waldo Milestein was a saint and that he would never in a million years threaten a woman simply to have sex with her," Raquel said, handing Ronnie a glass of her favorite drink of scotch and water before pouring herself a glass of white wine.

They walked over to seat themselves on one of the stools surrounding the island.

"I think it went well. Also, as far as what those in Hollywood think of the interview, I could not care less. They are going to believe what they want to believe, and no amount of truth is going to change their minds."

"All I can say is I am very proud of the way you handled the interview. You were able to set straight all the silliness being spread by the Hollywood morons." She suddenly becomes silent as she stares straight ahead.

"Mother, what is it?" Ronnie turns to see what is wrong.

"I just saw that crystal liquor decanter lift and then go back down. "Her voice takes on a trembling tone as she continues to stare over at the small bar.

"Probably the lighting. I thought I've seen

things over near the bar too, and it was nothing. You mustn't allow those wild stories of Uncle Cory's to go to your head, else people will accuse you of starting into your dotage, and we know that isn't so."

Ronnie hated to use her mother's age to get her off the thought that she may have seen something in the house, but she had no choice.

"Yes, I am sure you're right, Ronnie. It has been a long day and an exciting evening. I think I should be heading home and relax in the hot tub for a while."

"Sounds like a great idea. And you might want to drag that handsome husband of yours into the hot tub with you. That will relax you even more." Ronnie laughs aloud as she sees the embarrassed flush covering her mother's pretty face.

"Yes, I think that is a great idea," Raquel admitted before drinking the last of her drink and getting to her feet.

Ronnie waves her mother off as she drives down the lane, then turns to go back into the house.

"All right, Leonard, you were told to not show up here this evening. Either you will abide by my rules, or you will not be welcome in this house."

"You're blaming the wrong one here, Ronnie. I thought I could get a drink without anyone seeing me, but I was wrong, and I am so sorry for upsetting Raquel," Cory tells her as he materializes into full view.

Ronnie's hand goes up to her throat as she stares at the man watching her, then putting out her arms, she runs to him. "I know you would never do anything to frighten Mom on purpose," she whispers as she feels his arms go around her.

Cory laughs a deep laugh. "I wouldn't go quite that far, Ronnie. With her prim ways, Raquel can be a real target at times."

He leads her across the floor to the bar and pours Ronnie another drink, then one for himself.

"Don't put that bottle down yet," Leonard says, coming forward, "since I was blamed for something I didn't do, I feel I am entitled to share a drink with the two of you." The roguish grin crossing his handsome face is not missed by Ronnie.

"You best pour a drink for all of us," Jason tells him. "I say we all have a drink and go sit down and enjoy the quiet."

"I apologize for allowing Raquel to catch my lifting the decanter. I must tell you, Ronnie, I was very proud of how you handled that interview. I mean, you did not miss a beat no matter what question Flannery threw at you. I am sure you already know that you are going to be a target for all the sheep in Hollywood who will try to put you in your place. Even though they all know what a scumbag Milestein was."

Cory's gaze moves to include Leonard as he stands with his drink in his hand, watching him.

"It's good to see you, Leonard." He smiles as he holds out his hand.

"I was afraid you wouldn't come."

"Of course I would come," Cory says. "I would never refuse an invite to come and see how my Ronnie is doing and to spend time in my old house."

Leonard turns away. "I see," he nods, his voice little more than a whisper.

"No, Leonard, I don't think you do." Cory leaves his chair to come forward. "Had I known you were here in the house, I would have been here a lot sooner. I knew you had not crossed over, but I didn't know you were staying here in my old house."

"I felt closer to you here. And I feel that since I did not tell the Council of Elders that this lifetime I would be in a gay relationship, I have been afraid to cross over."

"Were you aware that you would be in a gay relationship this time on this plane?"

"No, not until I met you. Before that, I just thought I suffered from a low sex drive just as I did in all my other lifetimes when I came back into another life."

"Then you were not *intentionally* holding anything back while you were with the Council of Elders. They will not hold that against you. Now, when I leave to go home, you can come with me. Is this what you want to do, Leonard?"

Leonard looks around the room, then smiles as he brings his gaze back to the man watching him closely.

"Yes, Cory, when you leave, I will be by your side."

CHAPTER SIXTEEN

Ronnie removes her satin robe then sits down on the side of the bed. "It was good to see Uncle Cory again. His arms, when he held me, felt the same as always."

"Cory is a good man. He loves you very much, and he would do all in his power to be here for you," Jason tells her before sitting down beside her.

"I have a strange question to ask you. And please don't get angry."

"You can ask me anything you wish." His voice is calm and loving as he looks at her.

"Cory and Leonard were gay lovers while they were alive. Now that they will be going home to the other side together, will they continue to be together?"

"According to Cory, they will continue to be close friends; they will not continue to be lovers. Even straight couples do not continue to make love after they go home. Their strong affection for one another is not broken. However, the need to have sex to feed the libido is not necessary. A touch, a look, or just a loving smile is all that is needed to show that special someone they are still needed."

"Pretty much like the need for food and water, then. The spirit does not need to be sustained. Nevertheless, you did say that if someone wants to eat or drink on the other side, they can. Wouldn't that include wanting to make love, too?"

Jason smiles over at her. "No, lovemaking is only for those who are still in body."

"Until now," Ronnie whispers, gazing at the man who is taking her into his arms.

"Remaining on this side does have its perks."

"And for this, I am so very grateful. You coming into my life has made my world complete."

"Cory asking me to stick around here for a while to keep an eye on you is the best favor I have ever been asked to do."

"Guess we both owe my Uncle Cory big time," she told him, her breath catching as Jason pulls her to her feet and, reaching down, pulls her satin gown up and over her head to lay it across the foot of the bed.

"Talk about the lives of others can wait. Right now, I want to make love with the woman who holds my heart." His eyes peer into the watchful gaze staring back at him.

"Each time you are away from me, my heart is

filled with a cold fear that I will come home to find you gone."

He draws back to look at her. "Ronnie, you have my word on this. When the time comes, and I have to leave you, I will make sure you know of my leaving before I go."

"Let's not talk about that right now. I want you to make mad passionate love to me. Freeze my mind of all bad thoughts until all I can feel is your magical touch bringing me the satisfaction my body has come to crave."

Jason leans forward to run one hand down the side of her face, then inhales a deep breath as Ronnie pulls his hand to her hot mouth to run her tongue over the palm.

"I wish I was a gifted poet. I would have the words to describe the feelings you are bringing to my body."

"There are no words to voice how we feel, my love. There is only feeling."

Jason stretches out on the bed and smiles before a deep moan leaves his throat as Ronnie draws him inside. Seeing the smoldering gaze staring back at her, she slowly rotates her hips.

"Please don't stop what you're doing. I feel that if we take it slow, I can last longer and satisfy both of us more."

"Then I will do all in my power to grant your

every desire, My Jason."

"I have never experienced such soul-touching feelings. Now I know, for sure, that being in love has never happened to me in this lifetime."

Ronnie's sharp intake of breath rushes into the silence as Jason topples her onto her back. Leaning forward, he places an arm on each side of her beautiful face to gaze into her eyes.

"When you told me of your fear of coming home to find me gone, I felt such sadness come over me. You have taught me so much, my Ronnie. You have shown me what it feels like to be in love. What it feels like to make love and to care about not only my own pleasure but that of the woman I hold in my arms."

Ronnie reaches out to pull his face down to hers in a long and passionate kiss. When they draw apart, she pumps her hips up and down. Keeping the tempo at a fast pace until she feels the hot juices explode from his body and bring her own passions to fulfillment.

Jason moves his body to the side to pull her into his arms. "I thought my passions could not climb any higher, but each time we make love, I find I was wrong."

"I have never known such feelings as you bring to my body, my love. I think I could be content to stay here in your arms the rest of my life and let you feed my passions with your giving magic."

"This would be very good for me, but I don't think you could survive on love alone, my sweet one."

"I know, but it sure would be fun to try."

~*~

"I am going to have to stop enjoying a drink with you every night." She set the bottle of Scotch down on the bar. "There is enough sugar in this drink to ruin a model's figure, and if that happens, I will find myself out of a job real fast."

"I guess I am going to have to start chasing you around the property." He laughs openly.

"How kind of you to offer. I knew you were a keeper." She becomes serious as she hands him his drink. "If only life *could* smile on me, to allow me to keep you in my life, I would not ask for more."

"I know, and I agree with each word. We come back to this plane to perfect our souls and to learn lessons not learned in the life we lived before this one. But, I have to ask," a cold and cynical tone sounds in his usually calm voice, "what lesson am I supposed to be learning here? I get to finally discover what it feels like to be in love and care about someone?" A bitter laugh cuts the silence. "I am finally able to let someone into my life and put their feelings ahead of mine? What is the next step in this school of learning? I get to return to the other side without my heart? No! I refuse to do this! I refuse to throw away the one person who means more to me than anyone I have ever known just so I can put all my learning in my pocket to graduate top of my class when I return to the other side. Fuck that!" He disappears from her sight, leaving a stunned Ronnie standing where he has left her.

"Ronnie."

She turns as her name is called outside in the hall. Pulling her robe over her nakedness, she moves to open the door. Seeing Cory gazing at her, she runs to his outstretched arms.

Cory pulls her close against his chest, allowing her to cry out her pain as he holds her.

In his old familiar way, he runs a hand over her hair and smiles as she looks up at him, her trusting gaze locked with his.

"He is filled with so much pain. I don't know what to do for him. Tell me what I can do for him!"

"There isn't anything you *can* do for him, Ronnie. Jason knows he has *no choice* but to go home. He is simply prolonging what must be."

"Can you talk with him? Make him see..." she steps back, dropping her face in her hands.

"Yes, I'll talk with him. I know he won't listen to what I have to say, but I'll try."

"I feel as though this is *my* fault."

"No, Ronnie, if any fault is owned here, it belongs to me." He wipes a cupped hand over his face. "If I hadn't asked Jason to stick around for a while to keep an eye on you instead of returning home like he should have, this would not have happened."

"Uncle Cory, why is Jason feeling all this fear and anger now? When we made love a few moments ago..." she looks away, her face flushed with discomfort.

Tipping her small face up to his, he looks down at her. "There's no reason for you to turn away. Making love with that special someone is normal. Moreover, to be completely candid, needed to keep the mind sane. Ronnie, you know we have always been honest with one another. Now is no different. To answer your question on why Jason is filled with fear and anger right now, it's because he knows time on this plane is running out for him. Very soon, he is going to have to leave you and go home to the other side."

"Oh no, please don't tell me this. There has to be something I can do to keep him here with me. Why would our Father be so cruel as to let us find one another only to tear us apart?"

Corey takes her hand to walk into the living room to seat them both on the couch.

"Ronnie, now listen to me. You know I have never led you wrong. As you know, Jason is no longer a living entity. He is a ghost. He belongs on the other side, where his loved ones await his return. His trial, this time on this earth, should be over. You are a woman still living out her life on this earth, learning and making mistakes that will teach you what is right and what is wrong."

"Please don't preach to me, Uncle Cory!" Ronnie jumps to her feet to walk a short distance away. "Right now, I could not care less if I do right or wrong. If it would keep the man I love by my side, then the other side can be damned."

"What have I done? If what we've shared could make you feel anger at our Holy Father and the other side, then I have done you a great injustice, my Ronnie," Jason says, coming forward to pull her into his arms.

Unable to speak, Ronnie leans her head on Jason's chest as she continues to cry out her anger and pain. After a while, Jason leads her back over to the couch and gently sets her down.

"Ronnie, it is time Corey and I have a talk. I think you should stretch out and try to relax. We won't be long."

As they disappear from her sight, she closes her eyes, trying to calm herself, but the thought of Jason leaving, never to return, robs her of all her attempts to relieve her fears.

"I really messed things up this time," Jason says.

"Sometimes things happen that are out of our hands. In trying to make sense of why this was allowed to happen, even going beyond free choice, the only thing I can come up with is, before you found Ronnie and fell in love for the first time in your life, you were unable to know what it feels like to love a woman instead of simply using a woman."

"You could be right. All I know is I would give anything not to have to leave."

"Jason, you are not a stupid man. You had to know that eventually, you would have to leave here. I think the smart thing for all of us, who are out of body, is to go home. Ronnie is a young woman who wants to know the joys of having a husband and children. If you love her, Jason, you won't cheat her out of realizing this next chapter in her life."

"Yes, she has told me about her desire to be married and have children. You needn't worry. I love her too much to interfere with her dreams of having a family."

"She will miss you, but in time she will meet the man who is right for her and begin her new life. This is how life was designed."

"I know you're right," he slams one hand into the pool, startling a bird, perched on the side of the pool, into flight, "but right now, I would appreciate you not talking about the man she will meet."

Corey sees sheer pain showing in his eyes, and he turns away.

"You know you will be able to come back to

visit, just as I do, once you have been on the other side for a while."

"I'll pass. Even bound by spirit laws, after my soul has been cleansed of any wrongs I have done, I doubt I could see Ronnie with someone else and not try and shorten his learning experiences this time around."

"I see your point." Corey cut short the grin crossing his face. "And, too, if you keep coming back into her life, it will only make it harder on her to get over you and move on. Right now, I guess our talk is over. And, since I am no longer needed here, I will go and see if Leonard is ready to join me on the trip home."

"Now that Leonard knows he doesn't have reason to fear going home, I think he will go with you. I, on the other hand, won't be going with you. While I know all you have said is true, I think I need to give Ronnie a little more time to get used to the idea that I will need to be leaving her soon. And, I want a few more days to be with her."

Cory looks at him then, knowing anything else he can say will go unheard, walks away.

CHAPTER SEVENTEEN

"Whoa, somebody pulled an all-nighter," Dustin breathed as Ronnie walks into the studio.

"I was hoping it wouldn't show." She hastily pulls her compact from her purse to gaze at herself in the small mirror.

"No problem, my lovely one. I can have you back to your million-dollar model-self in no time at all." He pulls out a chair and gently sits her down. "Be right back."

Ronnie yawns behind her hand as she waits for Dustin to return.

"Good thing the ladies' room had no emergencies at the moment." He sets down a satchel filled with cosmetics and, unzipping the top, peers inside.

"How did you know that was in the ladies' room, Dustin?"

"Well, it sure as hell would not be found in the

men's room, at least by any of us *macho* dandies." He laughs openly. "But to answer your question on how I knew about this little magic maker, a woman can't go into the bathroom looking like hell and come out looking like she's worth what she's being paid without some help." Dustin continues to pull out the different cosmetics he is using on Ronnie until he withdraws a large mirror from the bag.

Ronnie takes the mirror from his hand to bring her reflection into view.

"I swear, Dustin, my good buddy, you are a wizard." A bright smile crosses her face.

"Thanks, but I have to give credit where credit is due and admit most of it was having something to work with. A woman as beautiful as you would have to go without sleep a hell of a lot longer than one night to be beyond reviving what *you have*, Ronnie." He piled all the bottles and lotions back into the satchel. "I'll let you return this to the right place in the bathroom cupboard."

"I can do that." She picks up the satchel to walk off in the direction of the ladies' room when Nichole steps into her path.

"Just the good friend I am looking for." She smiles, pulling Ronnie into her arms for a big bear hug.

"I can't wait to hear what you need this time, Nichole."

Nichole takes a step back, staring at her. "I don't think that was very nice, Ronnie. I thought we were better friends than that."

"I take it you have forgotten about the naked pool party you and your male groupies subjected me to after I told you I did not want any company that night."

"Oh, that was then, and this is now." She flutters her hands in dismissal of Ronnie's scolding. "Besides, I am sure you enjoyed the sight of all those gorgeous bare asses as much as I did."

"Nichole, there is an old adage that says, don't bullshit the bullshiter. Now, what is it you are leading up to this time?"

Ronnie continues on her way to the bathroom, knowing Nichole will follow her. After putting the satchel back in the cupboard, she gives the other woman a brief glance as she walks out of the room.

"Dustin, what outfit do I need for this morning?"

"Another stroll down Park Avenue wearing the same blue dress as before. I'm not satisfied with the other shoot, even though I can't put my finger on why. Something just is not right. I'm leaning towards the bored look on your face that morning."

"Maybe it isn't you. Maybe the problem lies with the model," Nichole purrs, coming forward.

"I doubt it, Nichole. You're a looker, but you're not a Ronnie looker and trust me, the camera is always right." Dustin turns away to begin setting up the new shoot.

"What the hell!" She spreads her hands wide. "If I didn't know better, I'd think I just walked into the wrong studio."

Walking out of the dressing room, Ronnie can't help but hear Nichole's burst of anger.

"All right, Nichole, so we can clear the air and begin our day. What is it you need?"

Seeing she has the attention of both Ronnie and Dustin, she smiles.

"That's better, and since you are both my co-workers and my friends, I want to invite you both out to dinner this evening at the best restaurant in town."

"That is very giving of you, Nichole," Dustin tells her, a broad snicker crossing his face. "Now all we need to know is what does the other shoe, you're about to drop, have to add to this good news?"

"Oh! You are such a smug little bitch, Dustin! I should withdraw my invitation, which by the way, includes your current crush."

"What's the occasion, Nichole?" Ronnie speaks up.

"The occasion is my current boyfriend's best friend, Rick, is turning 30-years old today, and he is not taking it well. Also…"

"Take a deep breath, Ronnie, because here it comes."

"Dustin, damn it, will you please shut the fuck up? I am trying to say something here."

"Nichole, you need to get out what you want to say. We are on the clock here," Ronnie tells her, trying to stay patient while not losing her temper.

"All right. Because it is Rick's 30th birthday, and as I said, he is not taking it well, I wanted to do something to make him feel better, so I told him a little white lie."

"Are we getting closer to where you are going to make your point?" Ronnie's voice is taking on an angry tone.

"I told him that you mentioned that night at the pool party how you think he is hot. I know, I know, but he is really down." She told them as they both stared at her. "And, to make sure he believes you really did say that, I told him that I invited you to be his date this evening at his birthday bash, and you accepted."

"You didn't."

"And you are surprised at this. Why?" Dustin walks back over to start adjusting the cameras, not bothering to halt his uncontrollable laughter.

"Nichole, I told you I am seeing someone."

"Oh, come on, Ronnie. It isn't like I am asking you to jump into the sack with Rick, although," she looks away for a moment, a light smile covering her face, "trust me, you would not regret it if you did."

Please, Ronnie. If you will do this one favor for me, you have my word I will never ask you to do anything for me again."

Ronnie gazes at her, and seeing the pleading look Nichole is bestowing upon her, she breathes, "All right. What time is he picking me up?"

"Ronnie, you are the best!" Nichole rushes to give her a big hug. "I will tell him you will be expecting him to arrive at your house at 7:ish. His birthday bash starts at 8:ish. I will never forget this favor, Ronnie."

"Don't hold your breath on that one, Ronnie," Dustin tells her as Nichole leaves them to change for the day's shoot.

"Nichole is like a little girl. She thinks everything she wants should be handed over with no questions asked.

"You are a good person, Ronnie. I hope this don't cause problems with your guy. Some men don't take kindly to their woman going out with another man."

Ronnie's breath catches in her throat as she thinks about Jason and how he will react to her going out with another man, even though it is simply an innocent favor for her coworker.

Seeing the uneasy look crossing Ronnie's face, Dustin squeezes her shoulder. "I think it's time for us to get to work."

CHAPTER EIGHTEEN

When Ronnie walks in the door, she sees Jason, dressed in swimming trunks, waiting for her, a bright smile crossing his face.

"I was afraid you might not be here."

"Ronnie, I told you I would not go home without letting you know the day I would be leaving."

He comes quickly across the floor to take her in his arms.

"My heart mourns the fact I will bring you sadness soon, but you know it can't be helped."

She pulls his mouth down to hers, wanting to lose herself in the warm feelings he was bringing to her senses.

Jason leans back to gaze into her dark green eyes. "Now, that is a greeting I could live with forever."

"I am going to have a drink. Are you going to join me?"

"Not having a drink in the evening was short-lived." He laughs. "The offer to chase you around the property still holds. Sure, I'll join you in a drink. Then if you want, you can join me in the pool. I wanted to wait for you. It is always more enjoyable when we do things together."

Jason reaches out to take the drink she holds out to him.

"I see you didn't bring anything home for your dinner. Aren't you feeling well?"

"Let's go sit down. I have something to tell you."

Ronnie sits down on a stool. After taking a long drink from her glass, she turns to look at him.

"Wow, it must be something serious. By the look on your face, I can tell it is something you are not happy about."

"You're right. I am not happy about the spot my coworker Nichole has pulled me into. Nichole has asked me to do her a big favor. She and her boyfriend are giving a friend of theirs' a big birthday bash at one of the best restaurants in town. It is his 30th. birthday and he is having a hard time reconciling the fact that he is no longer a young man in his twenties."

"And your friend, Nichole, has asked you to attend the party, and you think I will be upset that this will take time away from our evening. Ronnie, I have no right to want you to miss out on joining your friends in a fun evening." He leans forward to drop a kiss on her cheek.

"No, I know you would not want to alienate me from my friends. That is not your style. However, she told the birthday boy that I thought he was hot. Something I did not say and would not say. He was one of the men she brought along the night they all went for a bare ass swim in my pool."

"Ah, yeah, I do recall that night."

Ronnie looked at him out of the corner of her eye as he brought his drink up to his mouth.

"What I am not happy with is she told him I have consented to be his date this evening. She was so eager for me to agree to do this that I told her I would. He is picking me up at 7:o'clock this evening."

Jason threw the rest of his drink down his throat, and getting to his feet, he walked over to the bar.

"I see. Since you have already committed to go, you can't very well back out."

"Jason," she hopped off her stool to walk across the floor. "If you would rather I don't go, I will just tell him when he gets here, I've changed my mind."

"No, Ronnie, don't do that. You have a right to live your life without me always by your side. And I guess you might as well start now."

"Jason, if this is going to hurt you, I won't go. Nichole thinks the world and all who live in it owe her a favor. You are the one who is important here."

"Ronnie, one of the things Cory and I talked about last evening is my leaving. He pointed out how you want a family. You told me this yourself, so I know he is right. I can't give you that, no matter how much I wish I could. You might as well get used to living your life without me because the day is fast approaching when neither of us will have a choice."

She walks back over to the island to pick up her drink, only to set the glass back down. "I guess I better keep a clear head."

"Yes, when you are with someone you don't really know, it is never a good idea to be without your wits about you. Also, if something should happen, I can't be there, this time, to rescue you. The only time I can leave is to go home. Until then, I'm confined to this house and property. The hour grows late. You should be getting ready for your night out on the town," Jason says, moving towards the patio doors.

Walking up the stairs, Ronnie unleashes her ire at the one who is responsible for the tension surrounding her. "Nichole, if I had you here right now, I would black both your eyes so bad that not even Dustin could help you!"

~*~

At the sound of the doorbell, Ronnie moves to open the door.

"Hello, Rick, won't you come in?" She moves off to the side to give him room to walk into the house.

He smiles as his dark brown eyes move over her. "I would be a fool not to accept that invitation."

Ronnie finds she is impressed with his old-fashioned mannerisms as he holds out a beautiful bouquet of flowers.

"Thank you. Give me a moment to put these lovely flowers in some water, then we can be on our way."

Rick looks around, taking in the beauty meeting his eyes. "You certainly have a breathtaking home, Ronnie. And allow me to say, you look very nice this evening."

"Thank you and let me say, you look very nice this evening, too." She toys with the strand of white pearls complementing her black dress and matching black heels as her gaze skims over his neatly trimmed shoulder-length black hair, tieless dark blue, long-sleeved shirt, black slacks, and well-polished black shoes.

"I have to admit that the last time I was here, I was a little bit out of it…well, to be exact, I was a lot out of it, so I didn't get a chance to enjoy your place. I want to extend an apology that includes all of us who showed up, uninvited I've come to find out, for getting out of line that night."

"I would not have expected anything less since you all came with Nichole. We'll just move on and enjoy the evening. By the way, Happy Birthday, Rick."

"Thank you, and please let me say, I hope you are not going with me this evening because you were pressured by Nichole to do so."

"I have to say, Nichole did beg a little, but now that you are here, I'm glad I accepted her request to be a part of your special evening."

Ronnie finds she likes this handsome, well-mannered man standing before her, letting her know she has nothing to worry about by spending an evening with him.

Standing across the way, Jason watches as Ronnie and the man who is lucky enough to enjoy her company on this night disappear from his sight.

"And so it begins."

CHAPTER NINETEEN

Ronnie had forgotten how much she enjoyed dancing the night away in the arms of a handsome man and hearing the laughter of those relaxing with a few drinks and having fun. To her surprise, even the spoiled and trouble-making Nichole was behaving herself.

"I feel bad."

"Whatever for?" Rick gazes down at her as they move effortlessly across the dance floor in time to the well-played music playing softly in the room.

"I didn't get you a birthday present," she tells him.

"Yes, you did, Ronnie, and she is right here in my arms."

"Rick, I don't mean to throw a damper on your special night, especially since I am enjoying being with you this evening. However, I have to tell you, I'm in a relationship."

For a brief moment, he leans back, allowing her words to sink in. "Ronnie, while I appreciate your honesty, I have to tell you. Any man, and especially one who you're in a relationship with that doesn't have a problem with you going out with another man, has to be out of his ever-loving mind or on life-support."

Rick turns as he feels a pat on his shoulder.

"Time for the old switcheroo, Birthday Boy," Dustin says, holding out his arms.

"No problem, my handsome one," Rick tells him, pulling Dustin into his arms to dance him across the floor amid rollicking laughter from Ronnie and others in the room.

Without missing a beat, Dustin joins in on the fun and, to Rick's surprise, bends him to the side in a smooth dip.

"Okay, it's my turn to cut in," Nichole says, pulling Rick into her arms.

"The pleasure is all mine, Pretty Lady," Rick moves with her across the floor, only to stop, leaving his arm around her waist, as the band moves into a different tempo.

"Guess it's time to show these peasants what a real dancer looks like." Dustin smartly clicks his heels then reaches for a smiling Ronnie. "Come on, my beautiful wench, let's give them a show!"

Together they move to the throbbing rumba beat

without missing a step. When at last all the twirling, clasping, provocative-touching and seductive-gazing is over, they join hands and bow to the thunderous applause of those watching.

"That was one hell of a display of talent, Ronnie. The only thing missing is a flower clenched in our teeth." Dustin pulls her against his hip.

"You're not so bad yourself, my macho hombre!"

"I don't know about the rest of you, but I could do with a drink," Rick takes a smiling Ronnie by the hand, and together they walk back to their table.

"We need to hurry on over to Rick's table. They are about to bring out the cake," Nichole tells him. "Get your man and bring him over."

"You're talking to a real cake lover, Nichole. You don't have to ask me twice. We'll be there in a few minutes." He hurries off to find his date.

"I am having one of the best nights of my life, Ronnie, and it is all thanks to you. I guess turning 30 isn't so bad after all."

"Rick, you have nothing to fear. You are a very handsome man still in your prime, and I have enjoyed this entire evening with you."

Everyone gathers around as an impressive cake sitting atop a silver tray is placed in the middle of Rick's table.

Rick looks at the cake then bursts out laughing.

A picture of three muscular men facing the side of the pool, their well-toned assets bared for all to see, covers the top of a chocolate cake complete with creamy white frosting and a large lit candle with the number 30 centered in the middle.

"Nichole, I can't believe you did this," Ronnie drapes an arm over her shoulder to whisper quietly before giving in to her own fit of laughter.

"I want Rick to see he has nothing to be ashamed of. Any ass that looks that good is one to be proud of." Nichole leans forward to place a quick kiss on the side of Rick's face.

"Nichole," he pulls her in for a hug, "knowing you as I do, I should have expected this."

"Are you mad at me, Rick?"

"No, I am not mad at you. After all, you went out of your way to make this birthday one of the best I have enjoyed in many years," he tells her as he gazes across the table at a smiling Ronnie.

Nichole gives a slight giggle as she leans into the arms of the man encircling her slim waist.

Rick and Ronnie sit back out of the way of the waiters as they place plates and forks on the table.

"Would you like me to remove the picture and scrape off the frosting in the kitchen?" One of the waiters asked.

"No, that's fine," Rick tells him. "I can take care of it."

He lifts the picture from the middle of the cake and, turning it over, licks clean all the frosting from the risqué photo.

"He needs to stop! He's turning me on!" Dustin leans in close to his date, who slaps him a light slap to the side of his head.

"Couldn't allow anything that looks that tasty to be ignored." He flicks his tongue to capture a bit of creamy white confection clinging to the side of his mouth.

Ronnie gets up from her chair and, picking up a linen napkin, dips a part of the napkin into her glass of water. She moves around the table to wipe the frosting from Rick's face.

"You missed a spot," she tells him with a wink.

"Thank you. It's good to know I have someone looking out for me." He pulls the palm of her hand to his mouth.

Ronnie gently pulls her hand free to walk back to her chair.

"I think what began as a favor to me is turning out to be a favor to Ronnie," she whispers over to Dustin.

"You're reading too much into this. Ronnie is only trying to keep him from being embarrassed by having frosting smeared across his face," Dustin speaks up on Ronnie's behalf.

"I guess only time will tell." Nichole smiles

knowingly.

Eric, the man standing with his arms wrapped securely around Nichol's waist, offers his own opinion of what is going on with Ronnie and Rick.

"Rick is not a man who gives up easily when he sets his mind on something he wants. It is only obvious he is smitten with your Ronnie as anyone with eyes to see can see why."

Nichole rams him a playful jab in his stomach.

"I guess we will see how this all plays out. I think this time Rick is going to be disappointed since I know Ronnie is already seeing someone," Dustin informs him.

Nichole's date laughs aloud. "My money's on my bro, Rick. For the first time in his life, I think he has found the woman for him."

CHAPTER TWENTY

Ronnie walks into the house and is surprised to see no sign of Jason awaiting her return.

"Jason," she calls out into the silence. "Jason, I know you are here. You don't need to ignore me."

Her calls go unanswered.

"All right, have it your way. I am not going to apologize for having a good time. You said you would never alienate me from my friends, and I thank you for this. However, if you are going to sulk and try and make me feel guilty, you are wasting your time."

Dropping her purse on the island, she flips off the kitchen light to walk upstairs.

After removing her makeup, she pads naked into her bedroom and pulls back the bedcovers.

"Have it your way, Jason. The two drinks I enjoyed have made me happy and relaxed, so I am in no mood to squabble."

With that said, she stretches out in the bed, and

within moments, she is asleep.

Jason stands by the side of her bed, looking at her.

"It was not my intention to make you unhappy, my Ronnie. I want you to enjoy fun times with your friends. I am well aware of the fact that what you and I have entered into is not good for you." He turns away to walk out of the room.

The next morning as Ronnie is finishing her breakfast of yogurt and a cup of coffee, the doorbell rings.

Getting to her feet, she walks to the door fully prepared to tell whoever is there that she is not in the mood to entertain.

"Good morning to you, Ronnie," Nichole laughs, walking past her. "I decided that since Eric and Rick are going to be playing their usual game of tennis this morning, I would come over and see you and work out with a good swim in your pool. I would have called, but I know you won't mind having some company. In fact, why don't you change into one of your swimsuits and join me? I know you didn't put away as many drinks as I did last night, but you did have a few. So a good workout in the pool will benefit us both since we live off our good looks."

"I guess since you put it that way, I *will* join you."

Ronnie takes her empty container and cup to

the kitchen to dispose of the container and put the cup in the dishwasher.

"Go on out to the pool. I'll be there in a few."

Nichole climbs up the ladder to the high-dive and, inhaling a deep breath, dives headfirst into the crystal-clear water.

"How's the temperature of the water this morning? You don't look like it is too bad," Ronnie laughs as she climbs her way up the ladder. She jumps straight up on the diving board then plunges into the water.

"Ronnie, you don't know just how lucky you are to have a beautiful pool to keep you in shape."

"Yes, Uncle Cory is a real sweetheart to give me this beautiful house and land and pool. Trust me; I don't take any of it for granted."

"I had to laugh at Rick when I overheard him telling Eric how he knew he was going to have a hard time matching you money-wise."

Ronnie swam to the end of the pool to walk up the steps and out of the pool.

"I guess I am missing something. Why would Rick have to feel he needs to match me in anything?"

Ronnie pulls her small hat from her head to run a hand through her hair. Grabbing the towel she has thrown over a chair beside a small table, she begins drying herself off.

"I think Rick is enamored with you, Ronnie.

You are all he could talk about this morning when he came over to pick up Eric for their game."

"I am sorry to hear that. I told him the same thing I have told you. I am already in a relationship. Last night was simply a favor to you and something I don't plan to repeat."

"Are you telling me you didn't enjoy yourself last night? Anyone there could tell how much you were enjoying being with Rick. Any girl would enjoy being with him."

"Nichole, I didn't say I didn't have a good time last night because I did have a good time. However, I am seeing someone, and therefore I don't intend to damage what I have. Not for you or anyone else."

"Oh, cut me a break, Ronnie." Nichole squints up at her. "You are a grown woman, not a silly little teenager who believes she has to be true to the boy she is going steady with."

"Nichole, not everyone is a cheater. Any man I am with knows he can be sure I am with him and him alone. But if the relationship should come to an end, then and only then would I think about dating others."

Nichole pulls herself over the side of the pool, and grabbing up her towel, dries off. Then, leaning forward, she drapes the towel over her hair to twist it in place. "I have to hand it to you, Ronnie; you are one of a kind. While everyone else is glad to be living in the current century, you would be glad to have been stuck in the fifties."

Ronnie stretched out in one of the lounge chairs to gaze over at Nichole. "Are you telling me that being true to one man is not in your nature? I would think being aware of all the diseases running rampant right now would be enough to keep you from sleeping around."

"I didn't say that I sleep around, Ronnie." Her voice takes on a steely edge. "I just get bored with being with one man all the time. I like verity."

She stands eying the other woman as Ronnie continues to look at her.

"I am not trying to tell you how to run your life; however, it might be a good idea to let the man you are dating in on your choice of seeing more than a few men at the same time. Not everyone trusts that they're immune to killer diseases."

"And just in case you are ignorant to the fact that almost every drug store has for sale what they call prophylactics for men to wear when having sex. I make sure any man I take to my bed slips on that little rubber glove. So, I can rest assured that I am safe from any diseases."

Ronnie's stunned gaze moves over her. "You're admitting that although there has been extensive testing proving that even a pinprick in a prophylactic can allow the user and the one engaging in the sex act with the user to contract a disease including the deadly Aids Virus or wind up with an unexpected pregnancy?"

"Now, those are two things I don't want."

Jason sits quietly on the lawn beside the pool listening to their ongoing conversation, and fights to keep his anger in check over the man named Rick and his desire to keep seeing Ronnie.

"I think it would be best if we let this subject die a quick death. Suffice it to say, my evening out with Rick was a one-night outing."

"I wouldn't put money on that claim, Ronnie. I think Rick will have something to say about that."

"I think friend Rick best keep his distance and accept his time with Ronnie will not be repeated. If not, he will soon learn that an invisible foe is a foe best left alone," Jason whispers.

CHAPTER TWENTY-ONE

"Here comes my favorite girl. And of course, she is a vision to pleasure the eye even in the early light of morning." Dustin comes forth with his arms spread wide.

"Good morning to you, Dustin, my handsome macho male," Ronnie returns his hug.

"Was that a fun-filled night on the town or what?" Dustin leans back, looking at her. "I gotta tell you, Ronnie, now that I know what a great dancer you are, we will most assuredly have to do that again. My partner agrees. He was so impressed with our show of talent it was all I could do to talk him out of paying the band to play some more rumba music."

"We had them in our pocket." She giggles. "We were so spot-on we could tell what the other's next move was going to be." She paused in thought then continued. "Yes, Dustin, I did have a great time. However, there is one snag."

"Ah yes, the handsome Rick."

"Yes, the handsome Rick. Nichole has us all but exchanging vows at the altar. I have to say, though, he is a very nice man and a fun date. But, I had to tell him that he is wasting his time with me because I am already in a relationship that I do not want to get out of."

"The thing is, Ronnie, men like Rick are used to getting their way, and they do not take a refusal kindly. No," he holds up his hands, palms outward, "I am not saying he will not be nice when he gets turned away. What *I am* saying is he will not give up easily."

"A man with his looks won't be alone long. Also, I have to be truthful. Was I not already in a relationship, I would go out with Rick again. I enjoyed his company. He has manners that any girl would like."

"I am glad to hear you say that, Ronnie," Nichole pipes up, coming over to them. I cannot wait to tell you what Rick has in store for you and a few others. Including you and your adorable cutie, Dustin."

"I'm all ears," Dustin mutters, walking a short distance away to start setting up his equipment for the day's shoot.

Nichole glances at Dustin then goes on with what she was saying. "Rick wants all of us to join him and some friends at his home to enjoy a nice dinner and drinks this Saturday. He has invited a real chef to prepare the dinner, so we know it will be top of the line."

"Thank you, Nichole, but as I said, I am already seeing someone. Now it is back to the real world and my man. He understood about my doing you a favor by being a date for his merge into the 30s. Now I am back to being a one-man woman," Ronnie replies before walking away.

"I cannot believe she is being this difficult. Rick is a man any girl would love to date. Hell, even I dated him for a while, and I'll tell you what, if Ronnie only knew what a great lay he is, she would be foaming at the mouth to go out with him again."

"Ah, what can I say, Nichole? Some women, especially those who look like Ronnie and can have their pick of good-looking men, just find trustworthiness more important than a roll in the hay. Go figure." Dustin shakes his head, moving over to begin turning knobs on his equipment.

"Good morning, Nichole. I must say you are looking beautiful this morning," Mr. Rainier greets her as he walks out of his office.

"Thank you, Mr. Rainier. You are always so kind."

"It is easy to be kind to a woman who is as lovely as you."

Nichole puts her arms around his neck and, pressing her body against his, gives a little wiggle.

"I see our Ronnie is in fine form this morning, too." He gently pushes her away before turning to gaze in Ronnie's direction. "I still have yet to meet the man she is going with. According to Dustin, I guess it is getting serious."

Nichole sees the admiring look he is giving Ronnie, and her female jealousy rears its ugly head. "I don't think it can be too serious. She agreed to go out with my boyfriend's best friend on his birthday."

"I guess some women in today's world are into verity. However, I would not have thought Ronnie was the love them and leave them type. Maybe she was only going out with the friend to do you the favor you asked her to do. That is more like the Ronnie I know." He gives her a cold glance before walking to his office, closely followed by an annoyed Nichole.

Dressed in above the knee, short-sleeved white dress adorned with brightly painted spring flowers, Ronnie walks out of the dressing room to make her way across the floor to where Dustin is busily readying his cameras.

"If you aren't a sight to hold tight, I don't know what is." Dustin gives her the once over.

"Thank you." She strikes a pose.

"As soon as the boss fills me in on what we are going to be doing this morning, I can fill you in."

"Thelma had this dress lined out for me, so I guess the spread will have something to do with the new spring line."

"You are 100% right, Ronnie. We *are* going to be doing the new spring line today, Nichole tells her.

"You look very nice. I like the white dress with only the dark blue flowers instead of a verity. It complements your beautiful blond hair."

Nichole bursts out laughing. "Thank you, Ronnie. I guess *verity* is the word of the day. I was telling Mr. Rainier about you accepting a date with Rick even though you say you are in a relationship, and he came back with the fact that some women like verity."

"And knowing our esteemed check signer, I am sure he added that he doubts our Ronnie is that kind of woman," Dustin chimed in on the conversation.

"*Oh, kiss my ass, Dustin,*" Nichole informs him.

"I would, but I am already in a relationship, and like Ronnie, I try not to get into the verity scene too much."

Nichole turns her back on Dustin's sarcasm. "I had a little talk with Mr. Rainier, and I suggested we do something a little different with the photoshoot this time. And of course, he agreed that my idea is a good one."

"I don't doubt it, Nichole." Dustin agrees, a slight grin covering his face. "A businessman as smart as Rainier will never write a check for what he knows he can get for free. And, as if we haven't wasted enough time already, I see we have visitors."

"I am happy to say you are wrong on this one, our little fruit loop. The ones coming into the studio are more than simply visitors," Nichole tells him as she rushes over to greet two men coming their way.

"That looks like Rick and Eric."

"God only knows what the hell she's set up this time," Dustin breaths in an angry tone.

"Good morning, Ronnie." Rick walks up to stand beside her. "You are looking beautiful this morning."

"Thank you, Rick. What brings you to the studio on a workday?"

"No, no." Nichole moves forward. "Since this is my idea, I get to be the one to share the good news."

"I wish to hell someone would before I call it a day," Dustin declares.

"Since we always do the same thing with the spring line, I suggested this year we try something different. As we all know, spring is a time of renewal, not just with the budding out of flowers and shrubs but of couples spending time together out in the fresh air."

"Where in the hell are you going with this, Nichole?" Dustin steps from behind the camera.

Nichole gives Dustin a smug smile as she pulls Eric close to her side. "Where I am going with this is spring is the season of young love. Instead of just

Ronnie and me wearing the new spring line for the magazine, we need two handsome, well-dressed young men by our side to put out the message. And, as I told Mr. Rainier, who better to get the message out to the readers of The Over Twenty Magazine than two handsome men they can fawn over?"

"Hello," Rainier walks out of his office to hold out his hand. "I'm Mr. Rainier, the owner of The Over Twenty Magazine. I appreciate the two of you agreeing with Nichole's idea to do the spread. And you will be well-paid for your time."

"I knew you would see the originality of such a brave move, Mr. Rainier," Nichole says. "When the readers of The Over Twenty Magazine see the new spread, not only will they know that spring is in the air but more importantly they will know that love is in the air."

"Yes, so it would seem." He gives her a brief smile. "I see Nichole told you just what to wear for the photo spread. You both look perfect. Have either of you ever thought of doing modeling? You are both the right age for the magazine. Give it some thought then if you are of a mind to hear me out, we can discuss the particulars over a relaxing lunch."

"It would seem you and I are destined to spend time together," Rick whispers, his dark brown eyes overflowing with heartfelt admiration.

"I would say it is more like the interference of

someone who can't seem to keep her nose out of other people's affairs."

"Did I just hear a real Freudian slip here?" Nichole laughs.

"Before this gets blown all out of proportion, what say we get busy on what you want to be done here, Mr. Rainier?" Dustin declares, his cold gaze flowing over Nichole as she eyes Ronnie smugly.

"I agree. As we know," a bright smile slips across his lined face, "time is money."

CHAPTER TWENTY-TWO

Knowing Ronnie is not due home for a while, Jason avails himself of a relaxing few minutes in the pool. When he climbs out to move across the lawn, he sees two fresh drinks sitting on the table.

"Hello, Jason. I thought since our talk together is going to be one of disturbing truths, you might enjoy a drink to calm your anger."

"I thought you and Leonard were already back on the other side," Jason replies, dropping down in one of the chairs beside the table and picking up his drink drains the glass.

"You're right. We were. Leonard still is since his presence isn't needed for this visit. Too, since I'm the one who must be held accountable for this mess erupting in the first place, I keep myself attuned to Ronnie's safety while she remains on this plane."

"Why wouldn't she be safe? I would never do anything to bring her harm.

"While you may not *intend* to bring her harm, if you are unable to leash your anger at the man she spent the evening with on his birthday to do a favor for a coworker, you would still bring her unneeded pain."

"In case you have forgotten, Corey, I am bound to this house and property. I can't harm someone if I can't be near them." His cold voice fills with anger.

"This is true, and your point is well-taken, but if he should come here again to visit with Ronnie, what then? I must tell you, Jason, this is a side of you I have never seen before."

"The reason you have never seen my anger is that I have never felt such anger."

"Not surprising since you say this is your first time to be in love."

"You wasted your time in leaving the other side to come here."

"I don't think so, Jason. Why not play it safe and come home with me? Once you are surrounded with the Holy Light, all your anger will be gone, and Ronnie can get on with her life as she is supposed to do."

Jason stands looking at the other man before turning to walk into the house.

Having no choice, Cory follows Jason into the house and up to the bar.

"Do you want a drink before you leave? Seems

as though every time anything happens in this house, we all end up at the bar to throw back a few before we can get on with getting on."

"Yes, I will have a drink, and who says I am leaving? If you can have this much anger building in your mind, how do I know you won't turn this anger on Ronnie?" Cory gives him a brief glance.

"I could never hurt Ronnie. You can put your mind at ease on that."

"I wish I could trust that no harm will come to her if you remain here, but I can't."

"Looks as though we are at a standoff. I don't intend to go home at this time, and you can't seem to take me at my word that I am not remaining here to do harm."

"We both know I cannot force you to go home. You still have freedom of choice, and speaking of Ronnie, it sounds as though she just came home."

"Are you going to let her know you are here and why?"

"Yes, Jason, *I am* going to let her know why I am here." He watches as Jason turns away. "To do otherwise would be unfair to Ronnie."

"Jason, are you going to come to be with me this evening, or are we still sulking?" Ronnie calls out.

Jason materializes. "We aren't alone, Ronnie. Your Uncle Cory is here on a mission from the other side."

Looking across the room, she sees Cory standing just inside the glass patio door. Throwing her arms wide, she runs to him.

"What a nice surprise, Uncle Cory." She pulls him into her arms to place a kiss on the side of his face.

"It's good to see you, sweetheart," he tells her, returning her affection.

"We can all go out on the patio, and you can tell me all about your mission."

Seated around the patio table, Ronnie turns to gaze over at Jason.

"Are you in a better mood today, Jason? I hope so as you have no reason to be upset with me."

"Why don't we keep our private business between us, Ronnie?" Jason says, his voice taking on a sharp edge that earns him a sour look from Cory.

"This is what I have been talking about, Jason. It seems you can't keep your anger at bay even in the privacy of Ronnie's own home."

"What is going on here, Uncle Cory? Are you telling me you feel I am in some sort of danger around Jason?"

"This is what I am trying to determine. And until I am satisfied, I will not be leaving."

Ronnie stares over at Jason, waiting for him to speak up and put her mind at ease. When he remains silent, she sighs. "Jason, tell Uncle Cory that I have nothing to fear from you."

"If you have to ask, Ronnie, then I guess all those nights spent in each other's arms were all a lie. I told you that before I found you, I had no idea what it felt like to be in love." The pain covering his face tells her he means each word he is saying.

"We both know our moments together were not a lie, and I will not allow you to make them a lie." She leans forward, placing a hand on his wrist. "You are the man I have waited all my life for, Jason. I thought you felt the same about me."

"Whether he feels the same about you or not makes no difference. The fact remains Jason is a ghost. You are still in your body. You still have a path to walk, and as you have said, you want to have a husband and children. You cannot have that with Jason."

Jason pulls his hand away to get to his feet. "We both know all this, Cory, so you needn't keep beating on what is. Of course, I feel the same about you, Ronnie, and these feelings are the reason for my anger. I can't bear the thought of you being with someone else."

Ronnie goes to him and, without a word, takes him into her arms.

"I didn't realize your feelings for one another run so deep," Cory says.

"We know the time will come when Jason will

have to leave and go home to the other side, but until that day, we will be together."

They stand with their arms around one another's waists.

"I have done you both a very grave injustice. While I had no way of knowing things would turn out this way, I should never have intervened in another's life trial."

"I trust Jason, Uncle Cory. I know he will never cause me harm."

"Can you promise me that the man you went out with as a favor to your coworker will never have reason to come here to your home?"

Ronnie remains silent for a moment, then moves over to sit down at the table.

"Until today, I would have, yes, but now, thanks to Nichole, everything has changed."

"In what way have things changed?" Cory asked, watching Jason as he makes his way over to the table.

"She talked Mr. Rainier into having Rick, the man I went out with on his birthday, and Eric, his best friend, be on the new spring line for The Over Twenty Magazine. Furthermore, now that Mr. Rainier has met both men and seen how well they complement the new line, he is doing his best to talk them into being male models for the magazine."

"Which means you will be spending every day

with this man," Cory says.

"I am afraid so. Mr. Rainier pays his models top dollar. Only a fool would turn him down."

"How do you feel about this, Jason?" Cory looks over at him.

"There is nothing I can do. Ronnie is a model. This is her career," Jason tells him.

"Jason, we can both see how much this bothers you."

"Of course, it bothers me. Ronnie is a beautiful woman; any man with eyes to see would want to be close to her."

"Can you rein in your jealousy?"

"Damn it to hell, Cory!" Jason jumps to his feet. "I'm not a fucking monk! I am a man! A man who wants to keep his woman away from all the other horney men of the world."

"Jason, you have nothing to worry about. You are the only horney man I want to be with," she tells him, then laughs as she sees the look covering Cory's face.

"While I can see you think you have a handle on any problems that might arise, I am not as comfortable. I will be staying here for a while."

"You are not needed here, Cory. You are interfering in something that is none of your business," Jason tells him."

"Be that as it may. Since I am the one who is at

fault here, it is up to me to keep Ronnie safe."

"Thank you, Uncle Cory. You have always been here when I need you."

"Since you seem to think Cory needs to be your protector, maybe I *should* leave and go home to the other side," Jason tells her, a slight whine sounding in his voice.

He stands looking at her waiting for her to choose him over Cory.

At the weakness sounding in his voice, Ronnie can feel her aversion for a grown man behaving like a spoiled brat rise, and she allows her distaste at his behavior to spill forth. "Jason, if this is how you feel, then I agree with Uncle Cory; perhaps you should go home. You have turned into a very cold and cynical man. A man that I am not sure I want to have in my life anymore."

"I guess there is nothing more to say on the matter, Ronnie, except this. I will never forget you."

Reaching out, Cory gathers a crying Ronnie into his arms as he watches Jason disappear from his sight.

CHAPTER TWENTY-THREE

As the first rays of dawn creep into the room, Ronnie throws her long legs off the side of the bed. Leaning over, she picks up her robe to slip it on over her Lavender nightgown.

"I can already tell this is going to be a bad day. With all the tossing and turning I did through the night, I can imagine what my eyes look like this morning. This could be the day I knock Nichole on her ass for pushing her way into my life."

"I already turned on the coffee pot and poured your juice," Cory tells her as she moves into the hall.

"Thank you, Uncle Cory. You are one spirit I don't mind having around."

"I'll meet you downstairs."

After a cold shower to help her greet the morning, she dresses then applies her makeup.

"I can see some tale-tell signs of a sleepless night." Cory seats himself on a stool.

"Thanks for bringing it to my attention. I am sure I will hear more about how bad I look when I get to the studio."

"You know you will always look good to me, sweetheart," Cory tells her, his deep voice filled with love.

"Jason did not come to me last night. Does this mean he has gone home to the other side?"

"We can always hope, but I am not so sure he is gone. Jason doesn't strike me as the type to give up this easily."

"I still can't believe he would do me harm, Uncle Cory. He is not a bad man."

"Jealousy is a very lethal emotion, Ronnie. This being Jason's first time being in love, we can only surmise how he will behave. I am in hopes that in his next lifetime on this plain, he will have the good fortune to meet a woman who will fill his heart with love and give him an entire household of healthy children."

"I hope the same thing. Listen, I have no interest in Rick. Yes, he is a fun person to be with, but I would never trade Jason. I even told Rick I am in a relationship so he would have no illusions of anything happening between us."

"Except your coworker, Nichole won't give up on getting a relationship going between you and this Rick. She sounds like a very meddlesome young lady."

"A spoiled pain in the ass is what she is. She thinks the world is hers to command."

"Have you told her how you feel about her pushing her way into your private business?"

"Of course. Nichole could not care less what others think. She will do what Nichole wants to do, and the rest of the world can be damned. She even brought her boyfriend and his friends here to use the pool after I told her I did not want to have any company that evening. They availed themselves of all they wanted to drink, then they all took off their clothes and went for a swim in the pool. Since they were all drunk when they got here, it turned out to be a drunken, nude pool party. Rick was one of the men here that night. However, I must say, other than he and the other men getting more drunk and getting nude, they did not disrespect me in any way. The only one to show disrespect is Nichole."

"Yes, such parties were a frequent occurrence while I lived here," Cory replied, staring off into the distance. "Wait a minute. You're telling me your coworker brought men here to your home to get drunk and swim nude in your pool?"

"This is what I am telling you," Ronnie says, getting to her feet to pour herself more coffee.

"I think you have solved the mystery of why Jason has suddenly turned so jealous. This nude pool party was before you went out with Rick at Nichole's behest, am I right?"

"Yes."

"No wonder Jason is up in arms over your spending the evening dancing and drinking with the man celebrating his special night."

"I had two drinks. Neither I nor Rick drank enough to get drunk."

"Let me ask you something, and I want you to tell me the truth, Ronnie."

"I have always been honest with you, Uncle Cory. You know this."

"Were you not involved with Jason, would you find this man Rick, someone you would enjoy seeing again?"

As she recalled the evening spent in Rick's arms and all the laughter ringing out as everyone there chimed in on the happy evening, she smiled. "Yes. Rick is a very nice man. He treated me with the utmost respect. He did not even try and steal a kiss at the end of the evening."

"He sounds like a man I would like and a man I would trust to date my niece."

Ronnie glances at her watch and hops off the stool. "I need to get going." She rinsed her cup and glass, put them in the dishwasher, and grabbing her purse, she heads out the door.

"I'll be here when you get home, sweetheart, so

have a great day," Cory said as he pulls the door to behind her.

~*~

Rick is getting out of his car as Ronnie drives up beside him.

"Good morning," he tells her, opening her door for her.

"Good morning to you, Rick." She steps out of the car. "I see we are both trying to beat the clock."

"Yeah, my alarm clock let me down. Guess I better stop on the way home and buy a new one."

"So, have you and Eric decided if you are going to take Mr. Rainier up on his offer on the modeling job?"

Rick opens the door to the studio, and with his hand on the small of her back, he ushers Ronnie inside.

"We are going to be joining Rainier for lunch this afternoon. I guess we are all going to have lunch together. He asked if we would come in this morning for a few more close-ups for the magazine. Is Rainier an easy man to work for, or does he demand a lot from his models?"

"I find Mr. Rainier very easy to work for, and you will also be able to say the same about Dustin."

Rick laughs aloud. "Now Dustin is a man I can be around with no problem. He is someone who says what he thinks and does what he wants at any given moment."

"Yes, I think a lot of Dustin."

"Well, bout time the two of you showed up. Thelma is chompin' at the bit, so you best go on in the dressing room and let her show you what you will be wearing this beautiful sunny day."

"How's it going, Dustin? You sound like you are in a jolly good mood." Rick gives the other man a high five.

"With my line of work, I can't be anything but jolly," Dustin replies.

"I hear you. Has Eric shown up yet? Rainier wants us to get a couple more close-ups."

"I haven't seen him. I would guess Nichole still has him tied to the bed. With her temperament, I wouldn't doubt she even wears spurs when she's in the saddle."

"You could be right." Rick grins, before looking away.

Dustin gives an involuntary shudder.

Dressed in a very revealing bikini, Ronnie walks up to Dustin as he loads the camera. "Guess our shoot today will be beachwear."

"Ronnie, you should be considered a lethal weapon. Your body could cause a man to have a heart attack," Dustin fans himself with his hand before quickly stepping behind the camera.

"I have to agree, with Dustin, Ronnie. You are

one beautiful woman."

Ronnie bows and smiles. "Thank you both."

"Okay, buddy, I just got word we are both going to be in the beach shoot this morning. We will be dressed in swim trunks and standing by a surfboard," Eric says as he walks up to stand beside Rick.

"Where's your other half this morning?"

"She's in the dressing room getting a suit on. Holy jumping up Jesus!" he murmurs, staring at Ronnie. "What I wouldn't give to have that beauty hanging on my arm!"

"Are you sure about that, Eric?" Nichole walks up beside him.

Jerking around with a lopsided grin on his face, Eric gives the woman glaring at him a look of complete surprise. "You know I'm only kidding, baby. I knew you were there all the time." The bright flush moving up his face tells a different story.

Nichole smacks him with a hard slap across his backside, making him yelp.

"Take it easy, woman. You rode daddy pretty hard this morning, not to mention you forgot to take the edge off your spurs before playing rodeo again."

"Thank god *my man* isn't a ballbreaker," Dustin mumbles to Ronnie.

"You and me both, Dustin," Ronnie says as she spies Rainier leaving his office.

"Good morning, everyone. I will be brief since

I can see you gentlemen need to slip into your swim trunks for the beach spread. I would like all of you to join me this afternoon for a nice lunch. I am always glad to show my models and also you, Thelma and you, Dustin, how much I appreciate you."

Cory stands back, watching all those in the room and paying close attention to the man standing by Ronnie's side, his admiring gaze never leaving her face.

~*~

Ronnie laughs her way through the morning as Dustin goes out of his way to turn their job into a plethora of playful mischief.

Eric grabs a squealing Nichole and positions her atop his broad shoulders.

"Yes, that is the look I am trying to get," Dustin calls out. "Rick, you need to put Ronnie atop your shoulders, and someone needs to hand her the beach ball."

Rainier laughs as he reaches up the beach ball to Ronnie. "Here you go, Ronnie. Dustin," he turns his attention to the man behind the camera, "your wanting to move this shoot to the beach borders on brilliance! I will be adding some well-deserved numbers to your paychecks from now on."

"I appreciate you taking notice of my genius since it's a given that anything I offer up is a keeper," Dustin calls out as the camera clicks away on one great shot after another. "Too bad the surfboards are just for show. Be nice if some surfers were out tearin' up the waves. They're really comin' in this morning."

"Then allow me to make your day, my handsome friend," Rick says, lowering Ronnie to her feet." Eric and I are both surfers. You should be able to get all the action shots you want this morning. How far out do you need us to go?"

"I think not more than 100-yards should do the trick."

"If the girls are up to it, I think we should put them back on our shoulders and show the readers of The Over Twenty Magazine our models are the best in the business," Eric says, grabbing up one of the surfboards."

"Nichole, I have to hand it to you. Your idea to go all out with this year's spring line is one for the books. I believe it calls for a hefty raise in *your* pay, also."

"Are you serious, Mr. Rainier?" She runs over, throwing her arms around his neck to give him a quick hug. "You are the best boss in the whole universe!"

"Well… thank you, but I have to say this time your idea is a multimillion-dollar keeper."

"I am happy for you, Nichole. And you too, Dustin. You both deserve the recognition you're finally receiving." Ronnie gives Dustin a thumbs up before pulling Nichole close for a quick hug.

"Yep," Dustin snickers as he peeks around the camera, "for once, you're not bein' a pain in the ass."

"And we know if anyone would know about a pain in the ass that someone would be you, our little tootsie-roll popper."

"I'll give you that one since today is our day to achieve."

"I trust you will make sure to keep a tight rein on the girls while you are on the boards. I have them well insured, but they are the best in the business, and I would hate for anything to happen to them," Rainier says.

"Put your mind at ease, Mr. Rainier. Eric and I are both pros when it comes to riding the waves."

~*~

"Now, aren't you glad I asked Mr. Rainier to hire Eric and Rick as models?" Nichole says as she and Ronnie are changing out of their suits.

"They aren't hired yet. This is why we are all going out to lunch so Mr. Rainier can talk with them." She hands her wet suit over to Thelma.

"You girls did a great job at the beach. But I must say, I am glad to be back to the studio," Thelma says, reaching out to take the suit Nichole is holding out to her.

"I agree with you, Thelma. I am hungry and anxious to go eat."

"I think you are starting to take a liking to Rick.

And I must say I don't blame you. He is a very likable guy."

"Yes, I like Rick, and I think if he and Eric agree to be models, I will enjoy working with both of them." Ronnie smiles over at her.

~*~

As the waiter leads everyone to a long table, Rick pulls out a chair to seat Ronnie.

"Thank you, Rick." She smiles up at him.

"You're welcome, Ronnie. Do you mind if I sit beside you?"

"Of course not. I already know what a good conversationalist you are."

"Now, if they only had a band, I could pay to play some soft music."

"You wouldn't make it across the floor before Dustin jumped over the table to pay them to play something with a rumba beat." She laughs softly.

As Nichole giggles behind her hand, she receives a gentle jab in her ribs from Eric.

After the orders are taken, and the drinks have been served, Rainier stands to tap a spoon against his water glass.

"This has been quite a day. I am in hopes I can finish it by bringing into our already great working establishment two very handsome male models that have already proven how valuable they are to The Over Twenty Magazine."

Dustin stands, and, holding his drink high in the air, he smiles at those seated around the table. "I, for one must say, as a cameraman, I have yet to meet two more handsome men as Rick and Eric whose relationship with a camera is phenomenal."

"Thank you for your input, Dustin," Rainier tells him before motioning him to be seated. "Now, as I was saying, if the two of you are ready to make a very good living, I am ready to sign you both to a very lucrative contract. After you hire an attorney, of course, to read over the contracts to be sure everything will be in your best interest."

Rick rises to his feet to hold out his hand to Rainier. "I would very much like to join such a team. An attorney won't be a problem, as Eric's brother-in-law is one of the best in the business, and he will be the one we will call on to go over our contracts."

Eric stands to hold out his hand in agreement with Rainier's proposal.

"The only thing that could polish off this day is to join Ronnie at her beautiful home for a few drinks and a lot of laughs," Rainier says.

"Are you hinting you want to participate in a nude pool party?" Dustin laughs.

"You have nude pool parties at your home, Ronnie? Why didn't I get an invite?" Rainier sits down and picks up his drink.

"Had I *known* there was going to be a nude pool

party, I would have rung you up," Ronnie tells him.

"You can still get a glimpse of what you missed if you can talk Rick into bringing you the picture that adorned his birthday cake," Nichole tells him.

"Now that," Rainier holds his drink high, "I will have to get a look at," he says with good humor.

"Would we be imposing to enjoy a few hours at your home, Ronnie? It has been a while since I have spent some time there," Dustin declares.

Mr. Rainier gazes at her, a hopeful look on his face. "I would love to spend some time in your home, Ronnie. The interview we did on the news didn't give us much time to spend there. Too, I would love to be able to look around. So many stories have been written about it. It is almost like a childish dare to prove the stories wrong."

"I'll tell you what. Let me get home and relax for an hour, then you can all come over. And Dustin, you can bring your better half if he isn't at work."

"You are the best, Ronnie. Now, let's enjoy our fine food and drinks," Rainier tells them.

~*~

Ronnie walks through the front door and calls out. "Uncle Cory, are you here?"

"Yes, Ronnie, I am here."

"I am going to enjoy a glass of orange juice, then I need to talk with you about something."

She takes a glass from the cupboard then turns.

"Would you like something to drink, too?"

"No, I'm fine."

When they are seated on the stools, Ronnie turns towards him. "I may have done something you won't be happy about."

"No, I have no problem with your inviting your coworkers to your home," he says, smiling as she stares at him. "I joined you in the studio today, then at the luncheon. Unlike Jason, since I have already crossed over, I can go where I want. Jason, as you know, does not have that luxury. Assuming he is still here."

"I wish we were able to know for sure if he is still here. He is in such an angry state of mind anymore; we can't be sure what he is capable of doing."

"As I said, I can't tell if he is here or not."

"Rick, the man I went out with on his birthday, will be one of the men coming over later. I certainly would not want any harm to come to him."

"Ronnie, are you finding yourself becoming fond of this man, Rick?" Cory watches her to get her reaction to his question.

"I don't know. All I do know is, I enjoy being around him. He makes me laugh, and I enjoy the laughter and the funny remarks made when I am with my coworkers."

"As I have said before, Rick sounds like a good man. I know you are a good judge of character."

"He is. I forgot how much I love being out where people are laughing and having a good time. This doesn't lessen my feelings for Jason. It is just that with Jason, anything that is done has to be done here."

"I can tell you are a little nervous about having Rick come here since we don't know if Jason is still here."

"To tell you the truth, I am not sure. Since I only knew the good side of Jason, I can't fathom him being evil. For anything to happen to Rick, that would mean we were both wrong about Jason. Without seeing it for myself, I could never believe Jason is a bad person."

"I will be here. So you needn't be afraid about having your friends come here."

Thank you, Uncle Cory. As I have always said, I can depend on you to keep me safe."

CHAPTER TWENTY-FOUR

"Since we were all coming to the same place, we just piled into two vehicles," Rainier tells her, his voice filled with amusement as Ronnie ushers them all inside.

"Sounds like a smart move to me."

"Good god, this is some place you have here. Your Uncle made sure the upkeep never lacked an experienced hand." He looks around as he moves through the house. "Would it be rude of me to ask if I could see the upstairs?"

"Not at all." Ronnie points him in the direction of the winding staircase. "I want all of you to enjoy yourselves while you are here."

As Rainier moves up the stairs with Dustin and his friend Dillard, Rick walks over to stand beside Ronnie.

"I agree with Mr. Rainier. You have some place here."

"Thank you, Rick." She makes her way over to the bar. "I am going to mix us all a drink, so you need to tell me your poison. Nichole," she turns her attention on the woman watching her as she stands with her arm wrapped around Eric's waist, "run upstairs and see what everyone wants to drink, please."

"I will be happy to grant your wish, Ronnie; Eric and I will each have a screwdriver."

"Rick, what is your pleasure?" She pulls glasses forward then opens the lid on an ice bucket.

"I'll have a scotch and water in a tub with a lime twist. If you have some lime, that is." He chuckles lightly.

"I have lime juice right here in the cupboard if that will suffice."

"Looks like you are not only a great model and proficient dancer, but a very capable hostess."

"Again, I thank you. If you keep throwing out such glowing compliments, you are going to give me a big head."

Coming to the landing, Nichole calls out the drink orders in a loud voice.

"If you like, I am a pretty good bartender, and I would be glad to help you mix the drinks."

"You're on," Ronnie tells him. "I'll put the ice in the glasses, and you can mix the drinks." She looks over at him. "I guess you are not only a talented model and a skillful surfer, but you are also an impressive bartender."

"Are we a great team or what?" He gives her a little wink.

His roguish kidding brings a slight smile to her face. "It is beginning to look that way."

As everyone troops back downstairs, Ronnie lines up the drinks across the bar as Rick pushes them forward.

"I am going to be enjoying my drink on the patio, and I hope no one minds, but I grabbed my bikini and also some swim trunks for you guys before leaving the studio. They are in this large bag here. They've all been laundered, so there is no need to worry about being attacked by crotch crickets. Thelma, I have a one-piece in here for you. So, I don't want to hear any excuses for you not being able to join in on the fun about to happen." She opens the bag sitting on the island to pull forth her suit then walks down the hall to the guest bathroom.

"Lord, I haven't been swimming in years. But right now, I am going to join in on the fun," Rainier says, grabbing a pair of trunks from the bag.

"Do we have a great employer or what?" Dustin laughs, reaching into the bag to pull out trunks for both himself and Dillard.

~*~

"Come on, Mr. Rainier, you can do it," Ronnie tells him, laughing as Rainier bounces a few light bounces on the high dive.

"Okay, but if I don't bob to the top within a few minutes, someone needs to come to rescue me."

"We got your back, and if need be, I'll personally give you mouth to mouth," Dustin tells him, an impish grin covering his face.

"Then, since I have nothing to lose and much to enjoy, here I go!" He bounced up one more time then dove headfirst into the pool. As his head clears the water, an ear-to-ear smile covers his face as he sees everyone standing by the side of the pool applauding his daring feat.

"I just had a thought. Since it's been enough hours for everyone to be getting hungry, I have a freezer filled with plenty of different meats, and we have a top-of-the-line grill; why don't we have a barbeque? A few minutes in the microwave should thaw what we need."

"That sounds like a great idea, and Dillard and I can run into town and pick up some different sides and buns to go with the meat," Dustin tells her.

"From the looks of your well-stocked bar, I doubt we need to stop by the liquor store. I *will* grab a few cases of beer, though. A barbeque is not a barbeque without a few beers," Dillard says.

"No need to get some beer. The bar fridge is filled with beer. You can check and see if the kind you drink is in there, though."

"Dillard is like me. If it's beer, it's just fine," Dustin tells them.

~*~

Seated in the front room, relaxed from a very successful barbeque and more than a few drinks, the talk turns to the very lucrative career of the previous owner.

"I am proud to say I never missed one of Cory's movies. He was not only over the top gorgeous, but he had to be one of the best actors to ever grace the silver screen." Dustin tips his bottle of beer to his mouth.

"I agree with you 100%." Dillard grins. "I must admit I had the biggest crush on Cory."

"Well, while I never had a crush on him, I certainly had a lot of respect for his talent as an accomplished actor." Rainier enters into the conversation.

Without warning, they hear a high-pitched yelp coming from the nearest guest bathroom.

"What the hell?" Rick jumps to his feet to move quickly down the hall. He raps on the door after trying the knob to find the door locked. "Eric, what the hell is going on? Are you all right?"

The door opens to allow an ashen-faced Eric to walk out into the hallway. "I had just finished takin' a piss when suddenly someone shoved me into the shower door. Thank god it didn't shatter."

Ronnie feels her stomach clench as she gets to

her feet. "Are you all right, Eric?"

"Yeah, I'm not hurt. But it sure scared the hell out of me." He moves across the floor to sit down beside Nichole on the couch.

Nichole pulls him into her arms to give him a warm kiss on his cheek.

"Oh shit!" Dustin looks around. "I bet it's the ghost Cory used to tell everyone about in his late-night stories."

"You mean those stories were true?" Rainier asks, the tone of his voice echoing his unease. "I thought Cory fabricated those stories to get this house into his latest movie."

"I'll be right back," Ronnie says as she begins walking from the room.

"Hold on, Ronnie," Rick says, walking over to her. "I'll go with you.

"I'll be fine. I am going to the bathroom further down the hall."

"In that case," he smiles and sits back down on the couch, "I'll wait here."

Instead of turning into the bathroom, she continues down the hall to one of the guest bedrooms.

"Uncle Cory, I need to talk with you."

"I am here, Ronnie."

She moves quickly across the floor. "Who is here? Is it Jason?"

Her voice fills with fear as she takes a seat on

the bed.

"I am beginning to believe that Jason has not gone over to the other side. I would guess that he simply wants to scare Rick and Eric so they will not want to return here."

"His shoving Eric into the shower door could have injured him badly."

"I agree."

Jumping to her feet, Ronnie calls out in a hushed voice. "Jason, I want you to leave my home. You are not welcome here anymore. We had a close and loving relationship, but it is over. You have shown me I can't trust you. You once told me you would never hurt me. You lied. You *have* hurt me, and I can't trust that you might bring me harm. Allow Uncle Cory to take you home to the other side."

Dark, diabolical laughter splits the silence, making Ronnie run to the protective arms of Cory.

"That tells me we have more than Jason here, Ronnie." He pulls her close as he looks around.

"Ronnie, when I told you I would never hurt you, I meant my words." Jason stands nearby, the look on his face showing his pain.

Instead of moving from Cory's arms, she looks up at him, trying to understand what she should do.

"Can't you remove what is here? You've been bathed in the Holy Light. That alone should give you the power to remove evil," Ronnie says.

"I can try. I need to see what is here. I know for sure we aren't dealing with a spirit. But whether it is a ghost or a demon, I can't tell."

"Uncle Cory, I can't live in a house that is being haunted with something evil. What am I going to do?" Her voice breaks, and she throws her arms around his neck.

"We know the Holy Light is stronger than the darkness of evil. I will have to confront what is here and see if there is more here than just one evil entity."

"There is only the one, Cory. It is the ghost of a man, and I know who he is," Jason tells him.

"If you know who he is, then tell us." Cory is finding it hard to keep the anger out of his tone of voice.

"It is the ghost of Waldo Milestein. He was evil when he was *in* body, and now that he is *out* of body, he is determined to wreak havoc on Ronnie and anyone who comes into this house, including me, whom he blames for causing his heart attack and ending his life."

"Well, can't we send him away, too?"

"Ronnie," Rick calls out as he gently taps on the door. "Ronnie, where are you?" His fear for the woman he is searching for, sounding strong in his voice.

Ronnie puts up a hand for silence before pulling open the bedroom door to see Rick standing in the hallway.

"I'm all right, Rick." She walks partway out of the room.

Rick pulls her into his arms. "When you didn't come back, I got worried."

"Thank you, Rick, but I'm all right. I just needed to do something before I came back out." She steps back.

Still keeping one of her hands in his, Rick moves further out into the hallway. As Ronnie turns to pull the bedroom door closed behind her, she sees the sad face of Jason standing in the middle of the room watching her.

CHAPTER TWENTY-FIVE

Surprisingly, Ronnie slept the night through with none of the fear she thought sure would keep her up all night, allowing her to greet the morning well-rested and ready to meet the day.

Everyone is already in the studio when she arrives, and as she walks through the door, their hands rise in greeting.

"Here comes the best hostess in the Pacific Northwest," Dustin calls out.

"Good morning, Ronnie." Rainier comes forward to give her a big hug. "I cannot begin to tell you how much I enjoyed last night's festivities. I haven't relaxed that much in years."

Returning his embrace, she laughs as she sees the broad grin covering his face. "I am glad you had such a good time, Mr. Rainier. I enjoyed having all of you there to help me enjoy the evening."

"After we got home last night, you were all

Dillard could talk about," Dustin tells her, pulling her close for a quick squeeze. "Even Eric getting' the bejesus scared out of him was not a put-off.

Ronnie turns away, trying to keep a growing fear from tightening her stomach.

"Were you able to figure out what all that was about?" Rainier asked. "There has to be a reasonable explanation as to why such a thing could happen since there is no such thing as a ghost."

Ronnie glances across the room in time to catch the wide grin spreading across Cory's face as he stands out of the way, in a far-off corner of the room.

"No, I still don't know what could have made Eric fall into the shower door."

"I didn't fall anywhere, Ronnie. As I said last night, someone or *something shoved* me into that shower door. You need to call a priest to come to do a blessing on your house. I think you have more going on out there than you know." Eric stands erect, not willing to back down on what he has to say.

"Sounds to me like Cory wasn't foolin' on the stories he liked to tell his late-night guests," Dustin speaks up, his voice low and etched with a sinister tone.

"Be sure and let me know if you come up with an explanation." Rainier gives Dustin a glance before turning away.

Walking over to the man standing beside

Nichole, who has one arm encircling his waist, she holds out a hand to him.

"I am sorry, Eric, for what you experienced in my home. I, like everyone else here, have no explanation for what happened."

Eric takes her hand to pull her forward, ignoring the angry look he is receiving from a jealous Nichole.

"I think we are all making too much of this." He laughs a slightly nervous laugh as he takes a few steps back from the beautiful woman anxiously, watching him.

"That is very *giving* of you, Eric," Nichole tells him, the condescending tone in her voice letting those standing nearby know how she feels as she puts her arm back around his waist to tighten her hold.

"Since there isn't anything Ronnie can do to change what happened and as Eric is willing to let the matter drop, I suggest we all get on with what we are here for," Rick says, coming forward, the laughter in his deep voice lightening the mood.

"I'll drink to that defusing suggestion," Dustin holds his coffee cup high in a toast.

"If you're smart, Nichole, you won't make a scene, now that everything has calmed down," Eric leans forward to whisper his warning.

At a slight tap on her shoulder, Nichole turns to find Thelma motioning her towards the dressing room.

"I have your outfit ready to put on if you are through here."

"Yes, I'm through. So, since I have been callously dismissed by the man I *thought* cared what I think, we can get on with doing what I am being paid to do." Throwing her arm down to her side, Nichole stomps off to get dressed.

"Don't go feeling sorry for her, Thelma. Nichole is a drama queen, who will wring every drop of pity she can wring if she gets to be the victim," Eric tells her quietly before walking away.

Later, as Ronnie walks out of the dressing room dressed in a stunning light blue halter-top, her firm and rounded breasts peeking provocatively over the top with a pair of short shorts of the same color, she sees Dustin motion her forward.

"We are going to be doing a summer barbeque theme. Summer is almost over, and the kids will be heading off to school, so one more all-out get-together should close out the summer spread in the magazine."

"You are so smart when it comes to choosing the right theme. I think Mr. Rainier is finally seeing what a gem he has in you."

"Speaking of gems, would you get a load of this one walking our way?"

Following his gaze, she sees Rick walking towards them dressed in a pair of tight cutoff jeans and a short-sleeved wide-collared white shirt tucked into the cutoffs and left unbuttoned to show off his dark coloring to perfection.

"Let me be the first to say, you look hot as hell, and I don't mean from the weather. You looked good in swim trunks, but somehow the shirt and cutoffs make you look even more manly and sexy." Dustin tries to quiet his breathing.

"Thanks, Dustin," Rick says, taking Ronnie's hands in his, "while I appreciate *your* views on how I look, I am most anxious to hear what *you* think, Ronnie."

Dustin walks back behind the camera, muttering, "What I wouldn't give to be the one to light up those smoldering orbs."

Ronnie smiles into his face as she leans forward. "I have to say I agree with every word Dustin just said, you look hot."

"So do you," he whispers. "Would I be asking too much if I were to stop over this evening, say about 8'ish? I could bring over something sweet, and we could enjoy a few drinks and maybe put on some soft music and enjoy being together.

His nearness and soft, enticing voice has her hungry body answering her needs. Before stopping to think, Ronnie nods her acceptance of his invitation.

"All right, everyone, gather around," Rainier says, walking their way. "We are going to be closing the summer layout for the magazine. Dustin suggested we go out on a barbeque get-together. Since this *is* what most young people do before heading back to school or college. I think this is the right choice for a late summer get-together. Too," he looked around at all his models standing around, "all of you look ravishingly stunning as always. All right, it is time to go to work.

As Rainier walks away, Ronnie looks across the room to see Cory motioning her forward. Pulling away from Rick, she smiles up at him. "I will be right back."

"I'll be waiting."

Cory steps from the shadows to take her hands in his. "Do you realize what you just did? My hearing is sensitive enough to overhear your conversation with Rick. After what happened to Eric while he was at your home, do you think it wise to invite Rick to spend the evening with you?"

She steps back, and her hand covers her mouth. "I didn't stop to think. I was so intent on enjoying a nice evening in the arms of a handsome man I forgot all about what we have going on now in the house."

"I suggest you tell him you would prefer the two of you go out to a club instead."

"Yes, that would be better. I will go do that right now."

As Ronnie leaves to find Rick, she sees Dustin staring into his camera and shaking his head.

"Dustin, is something wrong? You look upset."

"Who the hell were you just talkin' with over in that corner?"

"What do you mean?" Ronnie is well aware her voice is shaking, but she can't help it.

"In checking my camera, to make sure everything is working right before I start the shoot, I see a man of medium height move out of the corner and take your hands in his. *Then*, I can't see him at all. The only one I could see is you. Since he is taller than you, I should have been able to see him in front of you."

"You picked up Rick and me talking." She laughs a nervous little laugh.

"No, you and Rick were talking over here near me. The man you were talking with in the corner is shorter than Rick. Tell you the truth; he favored your Uncle Cory a lot." Dustin watches her.

"Oh," she thinks fast, "one of the custodians in the studio stopped me to tell me how great he thinks I look. I must agree. I was a little put out when he took ahold of my hands. Good thing he favors my Uncle Cory, or I might have told him off."

Before Dustin can continue arguing his point on what he saw, Ronnie moves away to go find Rick and change their plans for the evening.

CHAPTER TWENTY-SIX

Ronnie brushes face powder across her face, steps back to observe the effects, and, being satisfied with her appearance, turns to place the makeup back in her bathroom cupboard when a slight movement in the mirror catches her attention. She turns to see Jason standing in the doorway staring at her.

"You startled me, Jason. Do you need something?"

"I'm sorry I frightened you, Ronnie. It was not my intention."

"Did you need to talk to me about something?" She could feel her nerves begin to unravel as he stands silently watching her.

"Do you have a date tonight?"

"Yes, Jason, I do. I have a date with Rick this evening. He wanted to come here to enjoy the evening with me. However, as I am sure you are aware, that is out of the question. I cannot trust you or Milestein not to try and harm him."

"I would not harm him just as I would not harm you, Ronnie. I know you and Cory still believe I am the one who shoved your friend Eric into the shower door, but I can assure you it wasn't me."

"Before you became angry and jealous, I would have never entertained the notion you could harm me or anyone in my home, Jason. Now, I do not trust you, and I would never put someone I care for in harm's way.

"You say someone you care for. Are you saying since I destroyed the feelings you once had for me that now Rick is the new man in your life? I guess I wasn't that important to you, after all, Ronnie." The stark pain sounding in his voice almost makes her want to reach out to him, but instead, she turns back to getting ready for her evening with Rick.

A burst of laughter interrupts the quiet, making Ronnie spin around.

"You are not the great lover I was, Jason. If you were, this tempting little morsel standing before us would not be throwing you away for another."

Jason moves quickly towards Ronnie as she cowers back against the basin.

"You are not welcome here, Milestein. You need to go back to hell where evildoers like you belong," Jason commands loudly.

"You weak little nothing. You are no match for

me." The huge shadow moving forward emerges into the repulsive figure of Waldo Milestein.

"I disagree," the voice of Cory Williams enters into the conversation. "If I remember right, it was seeing Jason standing in the doorway that brought on your fatal heart attack and sent your evil soul flying out of your foul, disgusting body."

"How dare you take that tone with me! I am Waldo Milestein! The one, the Hollywood misfits, rely on to make them a star."

Cory laughs aloud. "You mean you *were* the one who made the Hollywood hopefuls flock. Now, all you are is a ghost too scared to go over to the light because you fear you will be sent to hell where you belong."

"I see no need for me to go over to the light, Cory. Satan is the one I worship. All those who give their soul to the dark side will be famous and rich and sought after. I should know." His eerie laughter fills the room as he disappears back into a dark shadow.

"Waldo, you ignorant wretch. I was one of the most famous actors on this earth. I did not give my soul to the dark side."

"I did not give my soul to the dark side, either," Jason speaks up, "and I was able to enjoy a very satisfying career as a stuntman."

"I am another one who did not give my soul to the dark side. And I could not ask for more than I already have," Ronnie says, beginning to feel more at ease knowing Cory is present.

"You bitch, I will teach you to go against me!"

At the extreme hatred in Milestein's voice, Jason jumps quickly in front of Ronnie and, in so doing, takes on the impact of the evil substance of Waldo Milestein.

"Oh my God, Uncle Cory, do something!"

"There is nothing you can do to help this worthless slug!' He deserves to see what he has taken on as someone who dared to go up against me!"

"I demand you remove yourself from Jason, right now!" Cory comes forward.

"There is nothing you can do for him, Cory. You have gone to the other side. Thus you know, and I know you cannot use your strength to save another soul. No matter how much evil I have done in this life, I am still a child of your God."

"He is right; there is nothing I can do. However, I can call on White Spirits to come and take him to hell where he belongs."

In an instant, the ghost of Milestein disappears from their sight.

"What have you done with Jason, Milestein? I know you can hear me." Cory comes forward. "You will bring him back here so I can take him to the other side."

"Jason is wallowing with all the other tortured

souls on the dark side. You cannot reach him. He must pay for ending my life." The voice of Milestein is heard in the tense silence.

"Can't you bring Jason back from where Milestein has taken him, Uncle Cory? Jason is not a bad person and does not belong on the dark side."

"I will need to speak with the elders. Only they can grant permission for a spirit who has been cleansed in the light to go to the dark side."

"What if Milestein tries to hurt me? He will know you are not here to protect me, and this is when he will make his move to bring me harm."

"You have no reason to fear Milestein causing you harm, Ronnie. You are protected. Your guides will be here to protect you. Milestein is too stupid to know about Spirit Guides. Spirit Guides choose to leave the side of the Holy Family where all is beautiful and safe to be with each child when he or she is reborn into this new life. All God's children have guides to protect them. Therefore, you have nothing to fear from Milestein. You are very protected. However, some, such as Milestein, choose to ignore any and all help except that of Satan, so their guides allow them to wallow in their evil until their spirit leaves their body to return home."

"How terrible for the guides to have to watch someone as close to them as their child destroy."

"Yes, I agree with you. It would have to be

awful, but since we all have freedom of choice, there is nothing they can do except stand by and watch."

"Uncle Cory, will you be in danger by going to the dark side by yourself? I am afraid for you."

"It is because I have been cleansed by the Holy Light that I will not be alone. White Spirits will go with me."

Knowing she could trust her Uncle Cory to know what is best, she gives him a farewell hug as she whispers a silent prayer for Father to keep him safe when he enters the dark side to rescue Jason.

CHAPTER TWENTY-SEVEN

She hurries downstairs as she hears the ringing of the doorbell telling her, her long-awaited night out on the town is about to begin.

Opening the door, she smiles as she sees Rick standing in front of her, holding a bouquet of red roses wrapped in dark green tissue paper.

"How did you know red roses are my favorite?" She takes the flowers he is holding out to her to bring them upward, inhaling their strong and inviting fragrance.

"Only a woman as beautiful as you would choose the flower of love for her favorite," he tells her, the smile he is bestowing on her making her reach out to him for a brief hug.

"I will put these in a vase, and then we can be on our way."

Rick follows her inside, and as she reaches for a crystal vase high on a wooden shelf, he moves forward to place a hand on each side of her slender waist to easily lift her upward to retrieve the needed container.

Ronnie laughs, holding the vase in both hands as Rick places her gently back on her feet.

"A girl would not need a ladder with you around."

"Any time I can lend a hand, you need only to let me know." His voice is low and sensual as he removes the tissue paper from around the roses and white baby's breath.

"Another thing we seem to be a team on."

"Allow me to put the roses in the vase. They have very sharp thorns. I would not want you to be harmed by anything I have to offer."

"Without stopping to think, Ronnie blurts out a question always, uppermost on her mind. "What is it you are looking for in life, Rick? Are you content to play the field, or are you looking to get married and have a family?"

"With the right woman, yes. And you, Ronnie? You have a very lucrative career. Most women in your position would not think of taking a chance on ruining a figure that affords her everything she could ever want in life." He spreads the flowers out then adds the white baby's breath before walking into the front room to set the vase on the large oak coffee table.

"I am not Nichole." Ronnie stands beside him.

"There is not anything I could want more than a good man to call my own and a good father to help me raise our children."

Rick turns, and before Ronnie can move, he pulls her against him to tip her face up to his. "It sounds as though you and I have been searching for the same one to come into our life." When his full mouth lowers to cover hers, Ronnie pulls his face down to meet his open mouth. Her own sensual hunger letting him know he need not be afraid to show her how he feels.

"It would be so easy to lift you into my arms and carry you upstairs, but I don't want to rush you. I respect you, and I want you to respect me, so I suggest we be on our way to our night on the town," he whispers, his warm, clean breath moving over her throat.

The fires spreading throughout her body almost make her forget the danger of allowing their desires to continue.

"I agree. However, I suggest we don't spend too much time in one another's arms on the dance floor, or we may be 86ed out of the establishment for putting on a show they were not prepared to share with their customers."

The laughter erupting from his throat has Ronnie joining him.

"Oh, now I know we are meant for one another. Anyone who can go from burning up with a desire to laughing about putting that spinning-out-of-control desire on hold is someone who has my everlasting attention."

"The only thing I can think of that could put a damper on this made-in-heaven love-match is the unarguable fact that the one who brought us together is Nichole. When she learns that we have feelings for each other, there will be no living with her," Ronnie tells him.

"You're right. However, Nichole is not a bad person. She is just a very immature person who believes she can live off her looks."

"I am not trying to bring up a perhaps, unfavorable memory, but she has let it be known you and she dated for a while."

"Yes. I couldn't put up with all the drama. When she started dating Eric, I thanked my good luck in having her off my hands."

"My heart goes out to Eric."

"Eric is the type of guy who will put her in her place. I think he is good for her. But enough about them, I am more interested in what lies ahead for us."

~*~

Seated beside him with the seatbelt pulled into place, Ronnie looks over at him. "Can I ask you a very personal question?"

Rick glances at her then backs the car out of the driveway to drive down the road. "You can ask me anything you want. You will find I am a very upfront man who is not surprised by anything."

"Or at least, you have not been surprised by anything thus far."

"Okay. Since I have no idea where you are going to take this questioning, I will agree and say I have not been surprised by anything thus far. All I ask is, if you are going to tell me that you were a man before you had extensive surgery to turn you into the most ravishingly beautiful woman I have ever had the pleasure of holding in my arms, please let me know now, so I don't pass out behind the wheel and stop a promising life."

Ronnie looks over at him, then busted out laughing. "You have such a way about you that makes me know I can tell you anything, and you will not look at me as if I have lost my sanity."

"I have a suggestion. Since I think what you want to ask me is serious, why don't we hold off until we have had our dinner with a relaxing drink already working its magic on our nerves?"

"I think that is a wonderful idea."

~*~

Seated in heavy leather chairs enjoying their drinks, Ronnie looks around the crowded room. "I have a feeling this is going to be our favorite place to come on our evening outings."

"I think you are right. This is the first place I

had the pleasure of holding you in my arms and the first place I heard your beautiful laugh."

She smiles at him over the rim of her glass.

"I guess the time has come for your personal question. So to save time, I will bring forth a few, perhaps, on your list. Have I ever been married? Yes. Was I a cheater? No. Am I a woman beater? No. Do I have any children? No."

"Do you believe in ghosts?"

He looks at her, expecting to see a teasing grin on her face, and when it isn't forthcoming, he leans back in his chair, staring at her. "Are you serious?"

"Yes."

"Does this have anything to do with what happened to Eric the other night at your place?"

"I am asking if you believe in ghosts."

"I've never really given it any thought. I've never seen a ghost or anything even weird, so I would have to say that no, I don't believe in ghosts. Why, do you?"

"Yes. Would you believe me if I were to tell you that yes, it was a ghost that pushed Eric into the shower door?"

"I don't know. While I know Eric well enough to know he would not make something like that up, not to mention he was too upset to be playing a joke, I still have to say I am not ready to believe in something only seen in movies. Why do you believe in ghosts?

Have you seen a ghost, Ronnie?" He motions the waiter to bring them another drink.

"Yes, Rick, I *have* seen a ghost. I have seen more than one ghost."

Ronnie can see the uneasy look crossing Rick's face, and she leans forward in her seat. "I know this has to be a surprising jolt since you are not a believer in those who have left their bodies. Trust me though, Rick, I am not losing my senses."

"I already know this, Ronnie, but I never figured you as someone who would believe in the supernatural."

Surprising even herself, Ronnie laughs. "I wasn't a believer until I moved into Uncle Cory's house."

"Are you saying you saw the ghost of your Uncle Cory in his house?" His voice is etched with his surprise.

"So there is no mix-up here. I didn't see the *ghost* of my Uncle. I saw Uncle Cory's spirit. A ghost has not transcended to the other side, whereas a spirit has."

"Sounds like you are really up on all this."

"When something is important to me and has an impact on my wellbeing, I find out as much about it as I can."

When the waiter has placed their drinks in front of them and has turned to walk back across the floor,

Rick leans in close.

"Ronnie, you said you were not a believer before you moved into your uncle's house, so this is all new to you too."

"Yes, it is," she tells him, beginning to feel uneasy as she sees the troubled look on Rick's face. "I have upset you, haven't I?"

"I wouldn't say you have upset me so much as you have sure as hell surprised me."

"Rick, I feel if we are going to have a relationship, then all our feelings need to be upfront. I don't like secrets."

"I don't like secrets either, but I have to say this is all mind-boggling."

"I can prove what I am telling you if you would like."

"I will have to give all this some thought. I don't mean to come off sounding like a complete coward, but I have to tell you, hearing from someone I am getting very close to, not to mention already lost my heart to, that something I have only seen in movies or read about in books could be real is making me very uncomfortable."

"I never meant to ruin our evening, Rick. I only want to be upfront with you about what we both will have to face if there is ever going to be a close relationship between us."

"What say, we put this off for now and just

enjoy the music?" He scoots back his chair to hold out his arms to her.

Ronnie gets to her feet and, taking Rick's hand, lets him lead her onto the dance floor.

CHAPTER TWENTY-EIGHT

"Help me!"

The terrifying scream echoing eerily in the surrounding darkness has Cory moving cautiously into the forbidding mist, searching for Jason.

"Jason, keep calling out. I've come to get you out of here."

"Yes! Please get me away from here! Oh my god, I am so frightened.

Cory reaches out. With a quick yank, he pulls Jason into his arms.

"Okay, Jason. You're all right now. I have you. I am going to take you home to the other side where you will be safe."

"No! I don't want to go to the other side yet. I want to go back to be with Ronnie." Tears fall unheeded down his face.

"Jason, look around you!" Cory shakes him in hopes he will listen to what he is being told. "You are right at this moment, on the dark side. Only evil lives here. Those who have committed mortal sins against our Holy Father and humankind are imprisoned here until they accept God and His forgiveness! You were sent here by an evil entity. You can leave at any time. If you go back to that house, you take the chance of being sent right back here by the ghost of Waldo Milestein! Is that what you want?" The anger in Cory's voice is heightened by his extreme unease.

"I don't know." His tone of voice holds the intense fear he is feeling as he looks around at the screaming souls twisting and withering on the cold stone floor as charred faces stare out at him.

"I don't want to leave Ronnie. I love her, and she loves me, no matter what she says now. Why can't you understand this? She has to know, after what we shared, that I would never harm her."

"Jason, look at me! What you and Ronnie shared is over and never should have been. Are you willing to lose your soul for a woman who does not care for you anymore? You need to wake up!"

"I don't know what to do!"

"Jason, I don't know if the Holy Elders will allow me to come back here again. If you don't come with me now, you may be stuck here for a very long time."

Hissing snakes curl around their legs as their blood dripping tongues lap at their faces. The putrid smell of rotting flesh coming from their darting tongues make both men try to turn away.

Jason screams as claw-like hands reach out, pawing at him, their sharp nails leaving a trail of bloody streaks down his arms.

"Look around you. The Holy Bible and men of God are not lying when they preach about sinners and those who denounce God being sent to the fires of hell. You are in hell, Jason!"

"Yes, Cory, I don't want to be here. I can't stand the sounds of their screaming and the screeching laughter coming from every direction."

He shudders as he looks into the hate-filled face of a man walking towards them dressed in a long, black cowled robe. His anger at the White Spirits gathered around Cory and Jason, showing on his face.

"Please! Get us out of here. I want to feel the loving arms of Holy Father holding me near."

"That is all I needed to hear." Cory holds out his arms to the White Spirits, who move quickly forward to gather both men into their arms to remove them from the evil darkness surrounding them.

CHAPTER TWENTY-NINE

Snuggled down in her bed, Ronnie tries not to think about what could be lurking nearby in the darkness.

"I wish now I had invited Rick to spend the night with me. It might have made more problems in the house, but at least I would not be lying here in my bed trying not to think about what could be watching me," she murmurs aloud.

"You have nothing to fear, Ronnie. I am here to protect you."

Ronnie sits up in her bed. "Uncle Cory?" She reaches over to switch on the small bedside lamp sitting on the night table.

"Oh, thank God. I was getting frightened. I know I can always depend on my guide, but I can see and hold you."

"Jason is safe in the Holy Light of Home. When he saw and heard what surrounded him on the dark side, he was more than ready to allow the White Spirits to take him home."

"Come and sit with me, Uncle Cory. I want to hear all about what happened while Jason was on the dark side."

"I would rather you not hear all of that. I don't like you being touched by evil even if it is only to hear about it second-hand."

Ronnie felt a slight shiver of fear slide over her at his words. "You are a very brave man to risk going to such an evil place, Uncle Cory. I am very proud of you."

"It was the least I could do since I am the one responsible for what happened between you and Jason. If not for my asking him to stay here to keep an eye on you, I believe he would have gone home to the Light a long time ago."

"You had no idea how things were going to turn out. You were just doing what you have always done. Making sure I was protected."

Cory pulls her close for a warm hug.

"I may have done something that I should not have done."

"And that something is?"

"I told Rick about my seeing ghosts. I feel that if he and I are going to have any kind of a lasting relationship, he needs to know what is going on in this house."

"Then you are getting serious about one another."

"Yes. Rick makes me feel good when we are together, and he wants the same things out of life as I do. A family."

"I am very happy to hear this, Ronnie. Rick is a good man. There is no doubt in my mind about this."

"I am going to invite him to come over after work. I want you to show up and allow him to see you."

At her words, Cory leans back, staring at her. "Are you sure this is what you want? His seeing a spirit with his own eyes could just send him running out the door with no intentions of returning."

"I asked him to think about letting me introduce him to the spirit world."

"What was his reply?"

"He said he would think about it. I could see he is not too hip on all this."

"Then perhaps you should not push him into all this."

"I have no choice." She lies back down in the bed. "I am going to live in this house, raise my family, and if the man I marry is uncomfortable here, then he is not the right man for me."

"Yes, that makes sense. Okay, I will do as you ask." Cory stands up. "You never know; he may not only get a dose of the spirit world, but he may also get to see a real ghost if Milestein wants to show his ugly face. Moreover, I would not count that out. Now you need to get to sleep. I will be here, so you needn't worry about anything."

"Good night, Uncle Cory."

Standing in the shadows, a tall form listens to the words being spoken and quietly laughs. "You have removed the one who cheated me of my life on this earth, but you have yet to stop me from being able to enjoy the destruction of the one who aided in that removal."

Cory quickly comes forward to stand before the shadowed figure of Waldo Milestein.

"You do not want to go against me, Milestein. Your soul is evil, whereas I have been cleansed by the Holy Light. You have only heard of the dark side and what happens to those who go there. You will not harm Ronnie or anyone else who enters this dwelling. If you try, I will have your evil soul thrown into the fires of hell.

"You cannot protect her each moment, even you know this. There will come a time when Ronnie will be at my mercy. And this time, there will be no one to stand in my way."

The shadow of Waldo Milestein dissolves, leaving Cory to stand staring after him.

CHAPTER THIRTY

"Good morning," Rick says, opening Ronnie's car door.

Ronnie smiles, getting out of her car. "Good morning to you, Rick."

"I wish I could give you a good morning kiss, but as sure as I do, we will be surrounded by everyone in the studio."

Without weighing what she was about to do, Ronnie moves forward and pulls Rick's mouth down to hers.

"I don't know about you, but I could not care less what others think right now."

Rick pulls her against him, enjoying the feel of her ripe body and hot mouth.

"There's a sight I waited long enough to see," Nichole says, a big smile on her face as she walks past them. "Carry on."

Rick places an arm around her waist as they

walk into the studio. "Good thing you don't care who knows we are getting closer. Nicole will not stop until she tells everyone here she was right all along."

"Then let's spoil her big announcement." Ronnie laces her arm around Rick's waist and tightens her hold. "Good morning all. Rick and I hope you are all having a great beginning to your day."

"Good morning to the two of you," Mr. Rainier says, laughing outright.

"Well, if this ain't a nice eye-opener, I don't know what is."

"We sure think so, Dustin," Rick tells him.

"Since all of you here are our friends, we want you to know Rick and I are dating."

"Did I peg this right or what?" Nichole laughs, spinning around.

"Yep, for once, it looks like you got the whole scoop right, my little news-buster," Dustin says.

Eric leans over and pulls Nichole close. "A bit of advice? Now that you were right, how about you let it go and stop patting yourself on the back?"

Nichole looks at him and, with a slight smile, plants a long kiss on his open mouth. "Thank you for the well-deserved compliment, my handsome bronco rider, and you will be glad to hear, I intend to do just that."

Eric glances over at Rick, giving him a quick wink.

"Hmm, I guess miracles happen after all," he whispers as Ronnie looks at him.

"Speaking of miracles, have you given any thought to what I suggested last night?"

"Are you referring to your introducing me to the spirit world?"

"Yes."

"If you're wanting to prove to me that spirits and ghosts do exist, then all I can say is I will trust you."

"Then I suggest that since you are of a mind to do this, can I count on you to come over later this evening?"

"Ronnie, I know you would never put my life in danger. If you say this is something I need not worry about, then, yes, I will trust you to prove to me that such things as spirits and ghosts do exist."

The repulsive face of Waldo Milestein leaped into her mind making her step back.

"What is it? You look upset."

"While I can still promise you that if you come over this evening you will remain safe, I do feel that it is imperative to tell you something that may make you change your mind about all this."

"I don't like the sound of this. If either of us is going to be in danger, I want to know what it is that can bring this danger about."

Ronnie glanced around to make sure they were

alone, and seeing Dustin already busy behind the cameras, she pulled Rick further down the hall.

"I am going to warn you about what you may encounter while at the estate."

"You are starting to talk me out of even giving this a chance, Ronnie." He can hear the unease entering into his tone of voice.

"I talked all this over with my Uncle Cory, and he promised me neither of us will be in any danger. But when I brought this up about spirits and ghosts, you asked if it was a ghost that pushed Eric into the shower door."

"And you answered that yes, it was"

"That is right, I did. The one who pushed Eric into the shower door was the ghost of Waldo Milestein."

"Okay. Let's say, for the sake of argument, that what you are telling me is true. My question to you is, why the hell would you want to live in a house that is haunted by the likes of Milestein? He was a filthy puke when he was alive, and now that he is dead, you're saying he can continue to wreak havoc on others?"

"He only thinks he can harm others. My Uncle Cory has given me his word that we will not be in danger as he is going to be there to protect us. As to why I would want to continue living in my house, even while it is being haunted at this moment with the likes of Waldo Milestein, the answer is simple. It is my house, and no one, including a ghost, is going to drive me from my home."

For a long moment, Rick remains silent, staring off into the distance. Then, inhaling a deep breath to steady his nerves, he takes Ronnie's hands in his.

"The last thing I want to do is lose you, so I guess we will be spending the evening together along with whatever else is planning on showing up."

"Spoken like a man who knows what he wants and refuses to allow anyone to stand in his way," Ronnie says, laughing aloud despite herself.

"Then I will pick up some fast food for dinner.

"If I was sure you were going to be able to stay the night, I would say that is a great idea." She moved closer. Smiling as he places his hands on her waist, "Then we could ride into the studio together in the morning."

"I don't know how any red-blooded man alive could turn that offer down and still call himself a man." Dustin laughs aloud as he passes by before turning into the men's bathroom.

"I have to agree." Rick places a quick kiss in the palm of Ronnie's hand.

Watching from his vantage point further down the hall, Cory nods his approval.

CHAPTER THIRTY-ONE

Rick places the paper bag filled with two salads on the island.

"What would you like to drink with dinner, Rick? I am going to pour myself a glass of orange juice. I think it is a good idea to keep a clear head this evening."

"I agree, and I will also have a glass of O. J. I am going to go wash up, so I will join you in a few minutes."

Ronnie glances across the floor to where Cory is standing and lets out a long breath as she sees him turn to follow discretely behind Rick.

"I sure hope I have made the right decision in all this tonight," she murmurs to herself.

She puts the salads on plates and places a fork and a napkin beside the plates before pouring the glasses of juice.

Taking a seat on one of the stools, Rick lets out a

pent-up breath. "So far, so good. The bathroom break was a success."

"Believe me when I tell you, we are both protected." Ronnie smiles over at him and picks up her fork to begin eating.

Without warning, deep, maniacal laughter filters out into the room, making Rick throw his fork into the air as he spins around on the stool.

"What the fuck is that!"

"That, Rick, is Waldo Milestein," Ronnie tells him as she reaches out, taking hold of his arm. "He thinks he is going to scare you into leaving me here alone."

"He better think again. Leaving you alone in this house is the last thing I will do."

Ronnie squeezes his arm. "I guess we can forget about enjoying our dinner. Let's take our juice and go sit in the living room."

"You pick the spot, and I'll be right beside you."

Seated together on the sofa, Ronnie takes a drink of her juice before setting the glass on the end table.

Rick turns his glass up and drinks until the glass is empty, then hands the glass to Ronnie.

"I guess we can't put it off any longer, so are you ready to meet my Uncle Cory?"

"Although I can't say I am ready, I have to agree we need to get the show on the road."

"Uncle Cory, will you come forth and meet the man I am anxious for you to get to know? I know you have already heard Milestein trying to frighten Rick out of the house."

Cory walks slowly into the room.

"Oh shit," Rick whispers. "I don't know if I can do this or not."

"Rick, you are in no danger. I am here as a favor to Ronnie."

"Are you a ghost or a spirit? I can't see through you. I am starting to feel as though I am being played."

"To prove my point, I will disappear and reappear, so you will know I am for real.

Rick sits back further on the couch and places his arm around Ronnie's shoulders.

Ronnie can hear Rick's sharp intake of breath as Cory disappears, only to reappear across the room.

"I guess you have made your point in being what you say you are." Rick glances over at Ronnie to see if she is as upset about all that is going on as he is.

"It took me a while to get used to Uncle Cory's visits too. However, I am glad he is here. He can protect us from anything Milestein can try and do to us."

"Ronnie, I think we should get the hell out of here while we can. This is not *even* in the realm of possibility." He begins to scoot forward on the couch.

"Rick, if you want to leave, I won't try and stop

you. However, I want you to know this. I am going to continue living in this house Uncle Cory willed to me, and I will not allow anyone or anything to change my mind."

Eerie laughter fills the room inciting Rick to pull Ronnie to his side as he rushes to the front door.

"Stop! I will not allow something as evil as Waldo Milestein to chase you from your home, Ronnie." Cory steps in front of the frightened couple. "You know I have always protected you. Now is no different."

Ronnie removes Rick's hand from hers to step forward. "I have always trusted you to watch out for me, Uncle Cory." She throws her arms around his neck and lays her head against his chest.

"And I always will."

"Ronnie, I can't deal with this. I feel as though I am in a horror movie." He shakes his head and looks away.

Ronnie disentangles her arms from around Cory's neck to face Rick.

"I trust my Uncle Cory to protect us, Rick, but if this is too much for you to handle, then I understand your need to leave."

"Rick," Cory holds out his hand to the man staring at him, his face drained of color and moving away, "Ronnie would never put your life in danger, and neither would I. Will you take my hand and allow me to talk with you?"

Rick looks over at Ronnie, and seeing the pleading look on her face, he moves back to the couch to sit down.

"I can't make myself take the hand of a spirit, but I will try and stay seated while you say what you have to say."

"That is all I ask," Cory tells him, seating himself in a chair near the couch.

"Rick," Ronnie stands in front of him, "will it bother you if I sit beside you?"

Rick reaches out for her hand to pull her forward.

When Ronnie sits down beside him, he places an arm around her shoulders.

"I can see the two of you are beginning to care deeply for one another. I am glad. I want my niece to be happy."

"I have never felt the way I feel about Ronnie with anyone else. She is the woman I have searched for all my adult life."

"I believe you. However, my question now is, do you love her enough to live with her in this house?"

For a long moment, Rick remains silent. Then taking a deep breath, he replies. "I have to admit, everything is moving too fast for me to say right now what I can and cannot do."

Cory smiles as he glances briefly at Ronnie. "I

appreciate your honesty, Rick. Instead of saying what you think *I* want to hear, you are saying what you feel in the deepest part of you."

Despite himself, Rick grins. "I have never been one to hedge my words."

Cory returns his humor. "I have never been one to hedge my words either, Rick."

A foul odor fills the air making Ronnie and Rick cover their nose as they look around.

"What is that terrible stench, Uncle Cory?" Ronnie gets to her feet, leaning into the strong arms of Rick as he pulls her to his side.

"What you are smelling is the stench of evil. Milestein is pulling out all the stops to get rid of the two of you."

"Can't you remove him? This is terrible. I can't have something this disgusting in my home."

"You are not strong enough to force me from this house, Cory Williams." The voice of Waldo Milestein filters out into the room. "I sent Jason Talbert to the dark side. I can do the same to Ronnie and her current stud. Do you want that?"

"As always, Milestein, you are behind on what is going on. Jason is no longer on the dark side. He is home where he belongs. The Holy Elders allowed me to go into the dark side with the protection of White Spirits to remove him. You can leave here and go home too. You do not belong here, Milestein. Allow me to take you home."

"Don't bother. I am happy here where I can punish Ronnie anytime I want. She was a willing participant in my destruction. She deserves to be punished. As for your inept stuntman, Jason Talbert, he should have gone to the other side the day he died instead of lingering here so he could be Ronnie's ghostly lover."

Ronnie looks up at Rick to see what Milestein's ill-chosen words are having on him. Seeing his hand still covering his nose, she drops her gaze.

"It is easy to *talk big,* Milestein, but you know and I know you are not brave enough to try and do anything to those in this house while I am around."

"You did not listen to my earlier warnings. I said you will not *always be around* to protect your precious Ronnie."

Cory laughs openly as he feels the hot anger growing to a fever pitch in the room. "You were all talk when you were in the body, and as we can see, you are all talk now. No one needs to fear you. I bet when all those in Tinsel Town heard the good news about your fat ass being dead, they went out and celebrated. In their eyes, Ronnie is a Hollywood celebrity after all."

Without warning, the ugly ghost of Waldo Milestein emerges into full view making Ronnie and Rick move across the room.

"I will destroy you!" Milestein screams, rushing forward, his hands reaching outward to encircle Cory's throat.

Instantly, four White Spirits move to wrap chains around the evil threatening to destroy the spirit of Cory Williams.

"Take him to the edges of the dark side and throw him in," Cory tells those watching him.

As she sees Rick drop down on the couch, his face covered with his hands, she moves to the bar to pour them all a much-needed drink.

"I will leave you now. There is no more evil here to threaten your wellbeing."

Ronnie places two drinks on the coffee table then reaches out to put her arms around Cory.

"Thank you, Uncle Cory. I know now I can remain here with no fear of danger."

Rick looks up to see Cory's raised hand as he bids them farewell.

"Ronnie, since I know you are in no danger being alone in this house, I am going to call it a night." He gets to his feet to stare down at her.

"If this is what you want to do, Rick, I won't try to keep you." Her heart tightens at his words.

"There is too much to think over, and I won't pretend that I don't still feel ill-at-ease here now that all this has come to light."

"Then I will bid you good night, Rick." She

reaches out then steps back as he moves out of her reach.

"Good night, Ronnie." He turns and, without another word, walks out the door.

CHAPTER THIRTY-TWO

Unable to sleep, Ronnie finally gets up from her bed to make her way downstairs. Walking into the kitchen, she moves to the cupboard to take down a glass to fill with ice and cold water.

"Hello, Ronnie."

Ronnie turns at the sound of a familiar voice saying her name.

"Jason." She stands where she is not sure what to do.

"I hope I didn't frighten you. If I did, it was not my intention."

"You look different, Jason."

He smiles over at her. "When a soul has been touched by the Holy Light, the soul takes on a glow of pure love."

She sets the glass of ice water down on the island and turns to walk towards him.

Jason encircles her in his arms. "You don't

know what being trusted by you again means to me."

Ronnie looks up into his smiling face to run one hand down his cheek. "I am happy we can be friends again, Jason."

"You will be glad to hear I am no longer the jealous and angry man I was before. While I still love you with all my heart, I want only the best for you."

Ronnie pulls away to pick up her glass of water and to walk into the front room.

Jason follows her to sit in the chair close to the sofa where Ronnie is seated.

"I can see something is wrong, Ronnie. You know you can share what the problem is, and I will listen."

"I know you will, Jason. I feel bad that I ever doubted you."

"There is no reason for you to feel bad. I was out of my mind with anger and jealousy. To put it mildly, I was not a good person."

"I thought I had found the man I wanted to spend the rest of my life with. To get married and have children, and I wanted all this to happen here in the house where I am happy."

"Why can't you have all this?"

"I invited Rick, the man I have been seeing, here to meet Uncle Cory and to learn most of what has happened here."

"This is understandable. If he is to live here with

you, he has to know about Milestein and the dangers he could be facing."

"Yes. This is what I had in mind. The meeting with Uncle Cory went well, but then Milestein wanted to make sure he was in command with what would and would not happen. He gave out with his eerie, maniacal laughter, which almost sent Rick running out the door. Then he appeared, allowing Rick to see him."

"I can see where that would be a shocker. What did Cory do when this happened?"

"Uncle Cory tricked Milestein into getting so angry that he tried to do Uncle Cory harm. Uncle Cory called on White Spirits to take Milestein to the dark side and throw him in."

"Good for Cory! Then, there should be no more evil to threaten you or anyone in this house. You should be able to have the dream you have wished for."

"Although Rick seemed not to hear what Milestein made known, I know sooner or later he will remember."

"Let me guess. Milestein let it be known about our being lovers."

"Yes," she whispered. "You have to agree that hearing that the woman you are talking about spending the rest of your life with had a love affair with a ghost is a bit unnerving."

For a long moment, Jason looks away then nods. "I will say this, then, I will say no more on the matter. I don't regret one moment you and I were together, Ronnie. That being said, I hope the man you have taken to your heart won't allow what happened between us to ruin what can be."

"I hope I am wrong but, I think it is already too late. When Rick left here last night, there was no question of his unease concerning this house. And too, knowing the house can be haunted by the spirit of Uncle Cory only adds to his unease. No, I strongly doubt he will want to live here. And, although this may sound selfish, I don't intend to live anywhere else."

"No, you are not being selfish. You love this house. In my opinion, if Rick cannot accept living here or anything else that has happened here, then he is not the man for you."

Ronnie gets to her feet and, reaching out, pulls Jason close for a long hug.

"Good night, Ronnie," Jason tells her, then steps back to watch her walk upstairs.

CHAPTER THIRTY-THREE

Driving into the parking lot at the studio, Ronnie feels her heart jump as she sees Rick's car.

"Oh well, maybe this is for the best. Better to get it over with than to be playing the "what-ifs" all morning," she murmurs aloud.

Ronnie gets out of the car then laughs as she feels herself pulled into strong arms.

"Good morning to you, Hot, Stacked, and Gorgeous," Dustin plants a loud kiss on her cheek.

Ronnie throws her arms around his neck to pull him up against her. "Dustin, you are just the person I needed to see this morning."

"While I do so enjoy your hugs, you're gonna need to back off some, Ronnie," he says. "You done woke my stallion, and he's ready for a bareback ride. Be a pal, and let me hold your purse." A bright flush moves over his handsome face.

"You never cease to make me laugh, Dustin."

As they walk into the studio, Ronnie looks around to see if she can spot Rick.

"Are you looking for me?" Rick asks.

Ronnie turns in his arms. "Yes."

"Then consider me found." He stands, looking down at her. "After the cowardly way I walked out on you last night, I was afraid you would not want to see me anymore."

Ronnie reaches up to place a warm kiss on his full mouth. "After all I *put you* through, I am surprised you still want to see me."

"You were simply telling me what to expect if we are to have a lasting relationship."

"I know trying to let those, who have never had a run-in with the paranormal, know what all can go on is not something to be taken lightly.

"Since we both know the studio is not the place to discuss this, why don't we go out to dinner after work and then go to your place and talk?"

A warm smile makes its way across Ronnie's face as she looks up at him.

"Yes, I would like that, Rick, because there is still something you need to know."

~*~

Relaxed by the good dinner and drinks they had shared, Ronnie pours them a glass of red wine to take into the living room.

"I think we need to keep a clear head for what I

am about to tell you, Rick."

"Okay," he says in a long-drawn-out voice. Seating himself in the chair across from the couch where Ronnie is sitting, his dark eyes are appreciative as they slide over her slender form dressed in an above-the-knee light brown dress and matching heels.

"When I first walked into this house with the knowledge it is now mine, I knew I would never want to stop living here. This is the house where I want to have a family surrounding me."

"I can't say as I blame you. This house is beautiful."

"I met the man I am going to tell you about on that first day."

Rick takes a drink of his wine, then cusses under his breath as he bumps the end table with his glass spilling a small amount of the wine down the front of his white shirt and dark slacks. He brushes the droplets off as best he can, then sits back in his chair, resting a foot on one knee.

"He introduced himself as a former friend and stuntman on some of my Uncle Cory's films. He seemed nice and respectful. We started spending time together enjoying classic movies and such.

"Sounds as though you had things in common. I can see how that would be an incentive to spend time together."

"Yes, I enjoyed those times. Then, I started to

wonder why he never arrived in a vehicle. So, I thought I would try to find where he was living since he said he had a place further back beyond my property. I drove around for a while but came up empty."

"You would think he would have told you exactly where his place was."

"Yes, I thought so too.

"Isn't he the one who helped you that night Milestein showed up unexpectedly? That had to be terrible for you. I wish I could have been here to protect you. I get angry just thinking about that tub of lard putting his filthy hands on you."

"In all honesty, I did think he was going to kill me. He said he would kill me if I didn't do what he told me to do."

Rick moved from his chair to take Ronnie into his arms.

"If Jason had not shown up when he did, I do believe I would not be here today."

Rick ran a comforting hand over Ronnie's hair and placed a warm kiss on the side of her face.

"I hope I can meet Jason someday and thank him for being here for you, Ronnie."

Ronnie leaned back and laid her head on the back of the couch. "It wasn't long after I met Jason that I began having very vivid dreams. I dreamed of being held and protected by loving arms. And, the one holding me and protecting me each night was Jason."

"I don't find it strange, given you enjoyed each other's company, that you would have dreams about being held and protected by the one you liked being with."

"Yes, except the dreams didn't stop at only being held and protected. They took on a deeper closeness."

She glanced up at Rick to see how he was taking what she was telling him.

"What I am saying is…"

"What you are saying is the dreams turned into the two of you having sex."

"Yes."

"Ronnie, I don't think you need to go into detail about your dreams and to tell you the truth, I don't care to hear about your dreams. I would venture to guess that everyone has had what is referred to as a wet dream at one time or another in his or her life. So, there is no reason for you to feel the need to tell me about this."

"Rick," she said, getting up from the couch, "I am going to fix myself a drink. Do you want me to fix you one, too?

"Sounds like this is not just about wet dreams." He glances up at her. "Yes, I think a drink would be very nice right about now."

Ronnie walks across the room to the bar. As she removes the stopper from the age-old decanter, she feels her handshake, and she sets the decanter down for a moment wanting to be sure she would not accidentally drop the beautiful antique. When she feels she can continue, she pours them both a strong drink and after adding ice to the filled glasses, she carries them to the living room where Rick sits watching her.

Rick accepts the glass she holds out to him, and after taking a drink, he sets the glass down on the end table.

"Ronnie, I think we have said enough about the relationship you had with this man named...Jason." His voice deepens. "I do not want to hear the details. It is normal to have dreams about someone you care about. Everything you are telling me is normal. So let's just leave it at that since there is nothing more you need to add to this."

Ronnie brings the filled glass to her mouth and drinks until the glass is empty.

Rick glances over at her, an astonished look covering his face.

"I wish I *could* agree that we can leave it there, but I can't. You see, Rick, what I am trying to say is, Jason Talbert was not just my dream lover. He was also my lover in my waking moments. And that is something that does not happen to a girl every day."

"And why not? You and Jason are both adults, so it was up to you to say what you can and can't do."

you down to da Bottoms, you can find some nice women down there."

"No, no, no, I want to go to Ledbetter Heights," the man replied. "And it's not like that; I'm looking for an older woman. Someone that might have lived here years ago. Here's the address I was given." He handed the cab driver a crumpled piece of paper.

The cabbie unfolded the paper and read the address. "That's da Bottoms, Ledbetter Heights now, named after Huddie Ledbetter. He used to frequent that area. That man was world famous and real talented. You heard of Leadbelly?"

"Yeah, the person I'm looking for might have hung out with him, or at least was influenced by him. Anyways I need to find her. I got something for that woman. The woman was a friend of my mother."

The cab drove down Interstate 20 weaving in and out of traffic. Cabbies must hustle. More clients mean more fares, and safety wasn't always their biggest concern. The traveler had just arrived from Africa and hadn't been in the States since he was three. He had spent the last thirty odd years trying to eradicate evil in the world. Roberto Barnum was a freedom fighter. His assignments now complete, it was time to catch up on his family, and the music they left behind. Most of it went unrecorded, or at least unreleased.

After receiving the package from his mother, he wondered if the woman was ever in the public eye. The man wondered how the hell this person was still alive.

He turned the corner onto the street in Ledbetter Heights and saw an elderly woman sitting in a rocking chair, on the porch of her two-story home. Mr. Barnum smiled, as the cab turned into the driveway.

The man paid his fare and left a hefty tip. "Wait here," he told the driver. "I want to make sure this is the right person." He questioned the woman. "Miriam Landry?"

She set her guitar next to the railing and took a sip of her lemonade. "Who are you?"

His eyes focused on her, while the older woman sitting on her enclosed porch wouldn't take her eyes off the man. She wore a plain yellow sleeveless dress, which hung below her knees. The wire-framed glasses were a little crooked, resting at an angle on her wide nose. Her gray braided hair fell past her shoulders.

He stood at the bottom of the steps, refusing to ascend until invited. "My name is Roberto Barnum."

Mr. Barnum glanced over his shoulder at the taxi still parked in the driveway. He smiled as Blues music played from the cab.

"My mother, Sara Barnum, was a friend of yours." She glanced up and smiled at him.

"I hadn't heard that name in about twenty years. How and where is she? Still in Haiti?"

He waved at the cab driver and gave him thumbs up. The taxi driver backed out of the driveway and sped off. "Well, I'm glad you are sitting. Mami passed away in the last coup. She was seventy when the military shot her. She still fought for the people." He carried a small package in his hand, glanced at it, then lifted his eyes and peered at the woman again. "She always wanted you to have this."

"Sara dead?" She rubbed her eyes a little while the man nodded his head. "Dey all dead now. Bo dead, Lightning dead." She grabbed her guitar and picked some blues. "My business partner, she dead too, Mojo dead,

4

"While what you say is true, Jason being my lover in my waking moments is where the abnormal part of this comes in."

"Ronnie, for Christ's sake, will you get to the point? I can see what you want to say is getting to you. But just say what it is you are trying to tell me, and then we can put it in the past where it belongs."

For a long moment, Ronnie sits looking at him, then taking a deep breath, she replies. "The reason this is so difficult to tell you about is Jason Talbert was a ghost. He was killed while being a stunt man in one of Uncle Cory's films."

"What the fuck? You are trying to make me believe you had sex with a man who was a ghost?" He draws back, staring at her.

"Yes, Rick, this is exactly what I am telling you. When Uncle Cory died and left me this house and grounds, he asked Jason to remain on this side to keep an eye on me. He never dreamed Jason and I would fall in love. This is the reason Milestein had a heart attack when he saw Jason standing at the front door. He and most everyone in Hollywood were at Jason's funeral, so there was no doubt in Milestein's mind that what he was seeing was the ghost of Jason Talbert."

Rick sits still staring at her before picking up his drink and bringing the glass to his mouth to drain the last drop before setting the empty glass back down.

"Every time I think I have heard all there is to hear about the goings-on in this house, you pull out one more bone-chilling event to blow my mind."

"I felt I could not hide something this important from you."

"What the...I mean," he stammers, unable to look away. "how the hell could a ghost even have sex in the first place? A ghost is not even functioning in a human body anymore, so how the hell could he even get an erection?

"Rick," Ronnie reaches out her hand, "I know this is all hard for you to understand."

"Hard to understand? How about impossible to understand? You are not making sense here, Ronnie."

"Rick, while I know this is none of my business, I want you to know my niece is not a liar. Nor is she someone prone to fantasies." The deep voice of Cory breaks into the room.

Rick looks up to see Cory standing beside the couch. "Even you have to admit this is very much out of the norm."

"Yes, it is, and had I had any inkling about it going to happen, I would never have asked Jason to stay here to keep an eye on Ronnie."

"Yes, I believe you were only thinking of Ronnie's safety."

"Thank you, Rick. I can see you are a man who speaks his mind and who, too, has Ronnie's best and Ray dead, and now Sara. Damn, all the people I used to know passed." She lifted her six-string and picked a new tune. "I guess I'm a survivor." She smiled at the foreigner.

The man handed her a box containing a manuscript. "I believe this is for you. We should read this together, so I can update it." She invited him in for some gumbo and lemonade and updated "The Lost Song of Miriam Landry."

"Do you have a record player?" He asked her as he reached into his duffel bag, pulling out a forty-five-rpm record. "Mami wanted you to have this back." He glanced around the apartment. A few pictures hung on the wall. Paintings of the famous bluesmen playing guitars on Maxwell Street in Chicago mixed with some photographs. Roberto noticed another a gold-plated item hanging on the adjacent wall.

Miriam smiled when she caught him eyeing the item. The man smiled as he recognized the song. A classic song from the sixties, played by one of the greatest bands of many generations. The band is still famous and sells out tours today.

She examined it and smiled. "No sir. Dat yours, keep the music live and kicking. Dat's da lost song everyone talking about. Do what you want wid it. It gonna make you a rich man."

"I ain't gonna do shit with it den. I'm sure dem publishers I dealt wid are gonna fuck us for royalties anyway. Those two white women I dealt with… I had a bitch of a time with them straightening your payments for, "Won't You Go Away". You should receive a higher percentage now." He started talking in the Creole accent Miriam never relinquished living for years in Northern

Louisiana. "It will just have to stay lost. I'll take care of it and pass it down the line."

He spent two weeks in Shreveport revising his mother's story. Miriam Landry, a survivor who didn't always use the greatest survival skills, accommodated the man. When he departed, he promised to keep contact with her. He boarded a plane for Dallas, then to London, finishing his journey in Lagos. He returned to West Africa to search for the roots of Miriam Landry's music, the roots of the religion which influenced her most, and to reunite with his lover—that's for another story.

Exodus 15.21 KJV
And Miriam answered them,
"Sing ye to the LORD, for he hath
triumphed gloriously. The horse and
his rider hath he thrown into the sea."

Chapter 1

The Runaway

1935, Morgan City,

Louisiana

Miriam Landry searched everywhere for a lost pack of cigarettes. She shook the quilt from her bed, swishing the patterned blanket back and forth. The pack of smokes sat in her bed somewhere. She swished the blanket again, then tossing it across her small bedroom to settle next her pile of dirty clothes. "Where dat pack of smokes I swiped from my mom?" The teenage girl said to no one in particular. "I must have left them dere." She cursed her luck, realizing she left the snipes across the canal at her father's place, listening to the Creole music he helped make famous. She eyed a tin of Perique pipe tobacco. Grabbing the tin and rolling papers, she tapped her feet and sang along to the sweet music coming from the front porch. In past days she joined the band to sing and play guitar. Other days she listened and sang from inside the house, or somewhere else on the property. Today's schedule was different. She made an appointment down-town and worried about it as her petite body trembled. The tobacco and papers disappeared into the pocket of her overalls and nestled against her chest.

The young Creole girl strolled towards the shop in the shrimp district of Morgan City, Louisiana wearing overalls, ripped at the calf, topped with a big straw hat protecting her from the searing Louisiana sun. At fifteen years of age Miriam Landry appeared only thirteen, standing five feet tall and not yet fully developed, so the boys and girls in school used to tease her about the bug bites growing on her chest. She wondered about hitting puberty since she'd been having her periods for about a year, and now her monthlies had disappeared for two months.

Miriam Landry—no one's fool and aware a baby developed inside her body, as she hurried towards a shop in the shrimp district. Mother Caulder, a tall Haitian woman from New Orleans who settled on the peninsula, ran her business with little competition. The residents, oblivious to her occupation, were aware pregnant teenage girls came in, and left no longer pregnant. Often, the young women carried a small burlap bag when departing.

Miriam rapped on the door to Mother Caulder's office. She paid attention to the rumors, that you knocked only three times. Townspeople said an old voodoo ritual required activities in odd numbers. Knocking on Mother's door more than three times makes spirits impatient. Miriam wasn't sure about the truth to this rumor. Tales get told, passed around and facts distorted as rumors exchanged amongst townsfolk.

The shop sat on the corner, adjacent to the barber shop on one side, where the shrimpers and oil riggers came in for their weekly shave and cut to talk about their wives and ponder about the prostitutes. A shoeshine stand stood between the two small offices. Three shoeshine men stood around waiting for the businessmen to show up to get their loafers polished up. No one came while Miriam waited. The shiners aged eleven to seventy flicked their rags like musical instruments. The rhythm of the shaking rags intoxicated Miriam as she tapped her feet with the guys. All the music on the peninsula hypnotized her.

Guidry's Tavern sat across the road. Miriam's father often played his zydeco music there, at least when he returned from touring. Today, she tried to stay out of the line of sight from Guidry's. She often attended her father's shows and didn't need to cause any attention across the street at the voodoo midwife's business.

Others waited for the businessmen, riggers or shrimpers to come in off the boats. The hookers paced around the corner and searched for any person requiring affection for an hour. They often hung out at Guidry's. Miriam's father met her mother at Guidry's. Prostitution wasn't amuck in Morgan City, but it happened, and the police and town council covered it up. The prostitutes were regular callers to the midwife, often showing up to get a homemade cure of what a client gave them, either a disease or an unwanted child.

Miriam smacked the door three times and waited.

A short and stocky prostitute strolled by and made a comment. "Wacha got the clap little girl? Doubt if any of these riggers wants to do you anyway. You are too little for these big boys. They'd shred you in two."

Miriam ignored the hooker, but her feet shook. The young woman commenced pacing. Stopping, she crossed her legs like she held in a pee. She reached in her top overall pocket, grabbed her tin of tobacco. Her hands shook in the breeze as she tried to roll a cigarette and strike a match off some flint. The match didn't light, and she walked around the corner to block the wind. Her hands continued to shake as she rolled the cigarette and she didn't realize she dropped the tin of tobacco she swiped from her father. An older black man with a straw hat walked by, grabbed it off the dirt street, smiled as he carried it away, and lit his pipe. The man lit the pipe in spite of the strong southern breeze whipping in off the gulf coast.

Miriam wasn't much of a smoker, unless nervous, then she used cigarettes to soothe her anxiety. She walked around the corner, to the shop entrance where Mother Caulder waited.

Tied above her head sat the dreadlocks the witch wore. Almost six-feet-tall and with her hair extensions she appeared much taller. In a slow drawn-out voice with a Haitian French accent she said to Miriam, "Where were you? I answered da door, and no one was dere. De conditions inside must be right for dis to be safe. Understand?" Her head tilted and she waited for

9

Miriam's response.

Miss Landry exhaled the tobacco in a ring away from Mother. "I's sorry Mother Caulder. I just gets nervous and wanted to smoke a cigarette while I's a'waiting. It's too windy here to light it."

"You knows dem tings ain't good for ya, and ain't good for no baby you be carrying. Now puts it out before ya come into my place." Mother Caulder spoke in a deep, husky and scratchy voice as if she smoked the cigs for a living.

"How's you knows I's carrying me a child? I didn't tell you nuttin'."

Mother smiled. It wasn't a cordial smile one expected while greeting a first-time client. She glared at the young girl like a she was a young, naïve country girl she'd seen a plethora of times before. She rubbed the mascara splotched around her eye and said with no remorse, "Why else you come to my shop?"

Miriam flicked the cigarette onto Canal Street and went inside before she caught the eye of the shrimpers and riggers. She didn't desire their greedy eyes or hands on her.

There weren't any electric lights or gas lanterns lighting Mother Caulder's establishment. The windows cracked open allowing sunlight in, illuminating the dark office. Candles sat everywhere throughout the office provided extra glow, and wafted a pleasant aroma, as Mother Caulder's business smelled like the spearmint chewing gum they make in Chicago. Miriam's nose twitched as she inhaled the incense burning. The aroma, undetectable to the teen, was reminiscent of the essence of the burning candles. Her demeanor resembled the rabbits she hunted for food.

10

interests at heart."

"Ronnie, I think I have had about all this I can stand for one evening, so I am going to head out."

Ronnie stands up from the couch and smiles as Rick reaches out to draw her into his arms.

"Goodnight, Rick. At least this time when you leave, we know we are still friends. I'll see you in the morning."

"Goodnight, Ronnie. We will talk more about all this." He nods to Cory.

At the door, he turns. "One more thing. In what films did Talbert work in?"

Closing the door behind Rick, Ronnie turns, "So, what do you take away from all this, Uncle Cory? Do you think Rick and I can work this out, or am I back to square one in looking for a man I can have a family with and trust to make me happy?"

"While I can tell that Rick feels a lot for you, I must say telling a man who has never dealt with the paranormal before that you had a love affair with a ghost is a bit much."

"I agree. Nevertheless, if we are to have a trusting relationship, where no secrets can enter in, I believe I did right in sharing what happened with Jason."

"Only you can make that call, Ronnie. You have always been a bright young lady. No reason I should start doubting you now."

"It's late, and I have an early shoot in the morning. If I don't want to look as though I have been on an all-nighter, I need to jump in the shower and then get to bed."

"I agree. I didn't notice the time."

"Uncle Cory." Ronnie stops him.

"Yes, my sweet one?"

"Thank you for being here this evening. Rick and I may not be able to weather this confession, but at least he can't say I haven't been upfront with him."

"I think Rick has a sturdier backbone than you give him credit for."

"I sure hope he can deal with all this and understand that sometimes things we never expected could happen, do."

~*~

Rick turns on the computer to bring up the movie list of Cory Williams. Choosing one of the last movies the famous actor starred in, he goes to the list of cast and crew. Within moments, he is staring into the face of Jason Talbert.

"I don't know whether to hate him or respect him for the part he played in protecting Ronnie from being harmed and perhaps even murdered by Waldo Milestein. I guess since he is no longer a threat to Ronnie's and my relationship, I will just be thankful he was there at the right time."

Switching off the computer, Rick gets to his feet,

and hiding a long yawn behind his hand, he flicks off the light in his den before walking down the hall to his bedroom.

Standing in the open doorway, Cory smiles to himself as he sees Rick pull back the thick bedspread of his queen-size bed.

"I don't think you need to worry about losing this man who has captured your heart, Ronnie. He cares more about your wellbeing than he does about a rare love affair you had with the ghost of Jason Talbert."

CHAPTER THIRTY-FOUR

Dressed in a rust-colored long-sleeved shirt and black slacks, Rick reaches out to remove a bright oak leaf from clinging to Ronnie's long hair.

"While it does look pretty peeking from beneath your dark locks, I don't think you want to walk around with a leaf in your hair."

"Wait!" Dustin calls out. "Leave it until I get a picture of it."

Mr. Rainier laughs aloud at Dustin's insistence on leaving the leaf where it is.

"As we are introducing the new fall line in The Over Twenty Magazine, I tend to agree with you, Dustin. A leaf landing in Ronnie's hair with the beautiful fall colors that match Ronnie's long dress works out perfect."

"This is what you pay me for, Mr. Rainier," Dustin says as he peeks around his camera.

"Yes, well.... I must admit you are putting it

together more and more of late."

"Hmm, Dustin murmurs, "I don't know whether to take that as a compliment or a dig."

"As well as this job pays?" Eric slaps down a friendly smack on Dustin's shoulder, "I would accept it as a compliment."

"No shit!" Dustin nods his dark head in agreement. "When you put it that way, I tend to agree."

Wearing a long, gold, and red dress with a slightly lighter gold color sweater worn over her shoulders, Nichole walks up and slaps a friendly smack across the seat of Eric's well-fitting dark slacks. "What are the two of you wild ones up to this morning that I might want to be a part of?"

"Just agreeing on how well our handsome bodies afford us a lucrative paycheck each week.

"I could not agree more. You look fabulous in that long-sleeved cream-colored cotton shirt and black slacks, Eric. All poor Dustin has to look forward to is coming to work dressed in tight jeans and a sweatshirt that hides a well-toned body that, if he were to play his cards right, could bring him panting compliments and afford him a handsome paycheck each week too."

"I'm happy with the money I take home each week, Nichole." His tone of voice letting her know he did not take her words lightly. "Not only that, the only one I care to have panting after my well-toned body already keeps me well-satisfied."

Eric gives Dustin a high five that brings a sour look coming forward across Nichole's face.

Thelma walks out of the dressing room carrying an off-white and gold scarf made of a lightweight material to hand to Ronnie.

"I think this would look very nice tied loosely around your neck, allowing the ends to hang down."

"I agree, Thelma, and the colors are just off-setting enough to match the tiny golden threads in the dress."

"I think this fall line is going to be a big hit in The Over Twenty Magazine this year," Mr. Rainier says. "I would even bet the teens will be pleased with what they see."

"Are we a happy group here, or what?" Dustin chimes in on the conversation.

"Yes, we are, Dustin, and with that said, I think we should all get together at my house this evening for drinks and pizza and laughs."

Dustin steps out from behind the camera. "Do you mind if I invite Dillard?"

"Of course, I don't mind. As I love to keep saying, we can't have a happy party if everyone isn't happy. Leaving a loved one at home alone would not be making you happy."

"I hope we don't have a repeat of the last time we were at your house," Mr. Rainier says. The unease in his voice letting Ronnie know he is not comfortable accepting her invitation.

"I think I can put your fears to rest on that one," Ronnie tells him, glad to see the look of relief flitting across Rainier's face.

"In that case, Nichole and I accept your kind offer to dine with you this evening," Eric tells her.

"Rick," Ronnie turns as she sees Rick walk towards them, "will you be joining us this evening?"

"You can count on it, Ronnie. I would be a fool to miss a chance to be with you," he tells her before leaning in close to whisper, "Should I bring my PJs?"

"I would rather you don't."

Rick frowns, beginning to turn away, then smiles as she pulls him back around. "I would rather you bring a hunger that we can finally satisfy."

Rick pulls her against him in a tight squeeze.

"Your wish is my fondest hope."

"Okay, you two, this is not the time to jump in the saddle." Dustin snickers. "We got work to do. We're being paid the big bucks, and I, for one, want to keep my checkbook happy."

"You tell'm, Dustin." Nichole laughs. "I have a strong feeling it's going to be a hot time in the Williams house tonight."

"For once, I have to agree with you, Nichole."

~*~

"As much as I enjoy having our friends visit,

I have to tell you I was glad when they took their leave." Ronnie leans forward to place a kiss on Rick's full mouth.

"I couldn't agree with you more. Although I knew it was not my place to suggest they be on their way, I was almost tempted to do so anyway."

Rick pulls Ronnie to her feet and into his arms.

"I am glad to see you are getting more relaxed here. I was beginning to fear the man I am falling in love with was going to walk away and ignore what we can share."

"Ronnie, let me put your mind at ease. I love you. I think I fell in love with you the moment we met. Not because of your beauty or your beautiful house and grounds, but because I could already see the good person you are."

"I am so glad we found each other. Now we can make our dreams of a family come true."

Standing across the room, Jason and Cory watch as Ronnie and Rick climb their way upstairs.

"While I don't regret what Ronnie and I shared, I am glad to see she has found the man she can be happy with," Jason says quietly.

"Yes, Rick is a good man, and he will take good care of Ronnie."

"I guess it is time we go home, Cory. Ronnie no longer needs to be protected, and we both have love-ones who await our return."